8 DAFFODIL RIDGE
& OTHER STORIES
BERYL TESO

CONTENTS

ACKNOWLEDGMENTS

With many thanks to my friends Janet, Sandra, Pauline, Gladys, Vikki, Heather and Tony as without their help and encouragement, my first story with all its faults (I hope not too many), would never have been written. A very special thanks to Diny who steered me through all the technical stuff that is beyond me, needed to actually put into book form.

No 8 Daffodil Ridge, Part 1

1946

George Williamson was on his way to visit his Aunt Millie. She was his mother's sister, but he had never cared for her as he found her rude and patronising to the less well-off side of the family – namely his, but he was stony broke and desperate through no fault of his own, and she was the only person he could think of who could help him out financially at this moment in time. He and his mother were her only surviving relatives, and they were to be her beneficiaries when she died. They had a copy of the will to prove it – unless the old witch had changed her mind.

'She's ninety five for God's sake, so how much money does she need for her remaining years. Was it too much to ask that she would give him an advance on his inheritance, or even a loan to tide him over until he got back on his feet?' He asked his Mother? She smiled at him; but knowing her sister she doubted it. She was the meanest person she had ever met, but she didn't tell George.

George had returned from the war after five years of constant fighting through North Africa, Italy and then in France as part of the D day invasion force. He looked as if he had come through those terrible battles unscathed, but this was not true. His scars didn't show, but they were there, buried deep inside him. The only emotion he felt was anger, but feelings of love, sympathy, even fear itself, he'd left behind on the battlefield at Monte Casino in Italy. The fighting raged on for four months with heavy casualties on both sides, and one of the first to die was his friend Eddie who was blown to bits. George had been lifted up by the blast and deposited a few feet away, but apart for a few bruises he appeared to be unharmed, but that was not true. His soul died along with Eddie that day.

'When I was called up, the bastards told us 'it'll all be over by Christmas' just like they had to the volunteers in the Great War. Liars the lot of them' he mused 'Fighting for King and Country? Oh yeah! For King and the privileged more likely, not the poor sods like Eddie who gave their lives, or others who were maimed and traumatised fighting for them'.

His anger and bitterness was not entirely aimed at the ruling classes. It had been brought on because he had been let down badly by someone he thought he could trust with his life. Before the war he had owned a thriving little ironmongers shop in South East London where he worked alongside Reg Wilson, a much older man who had been both his assistant and friend. When he had been 'called up' to serve in the army, Reg had promised to run the business for him until the war was over, and George had trusted him to do just that.

However, when he was demobbed and returned home, (dressed in his horrible bright blue ill-fitting demob suit, courtesy of His Majesty's government) he discovered that Reg had absconded with his stock and his money and had left the shop to fall into disrepair.

'Why didn't you write and tell me?' he yelled at his mother. 'You must have known what he was doing?'

'It never occurred to me that he would do such a thing, particularly when you were away fighting in the war. When I finally realised what he was up to, I didn't tell you because you were stuck in

France and couldn't do anything about the situation other than worry about it, and that would have put you in danger.'

'What danger? 'What'cher' mean?'

'Well you needed to concentrate on killing Germans not Reg, as that would have been a distraction and therefore dangerous in your situation. Anyway, she continued 'I went around to see him last January, and according to the neighbours he'd scarpered months before, so what could I do about it? I made lots of enquiries but drew a blank. I reported it to the police, but they were not that interested, but then -- what could they do? There was a war on and they had more important things to worry about than Reg Wilson.'

George was furious. 'How am I supposed to earn a decent living now?'

'Go to see Millie and see if she will help you out, after all we are her closest relatives. I can't think of any other solution to your problems at the moment' his mother suggested, although she doubted Millie would help. But not being able to think of any alternative action he could take, she hoped, her sister might just for once in her life help out a member of her family.

Aunt Millie's cottage was a long way from the station, and George was exhausted when he finally arrived. It was the last one in a terrace of eight ending in a cul-de-sac, and she owned them all. He rang the bell several times, only to be greeted by silence. 'Shit, she's out, but having come all this way I'd better hang on until she turns up' he thought, and sat on her damp doorstep to wait for her to return. 'I'm sure this is all very pretty in the summer he surmised,' but with heavy grey skies, the dripping foliage and the lack of any flowers let alone a daffodil, the ridge presented a gloomy picture. 'For heaven's sake' he thought, 'she's ancient, why on earth would she want to live in such a remote spot right at the end of the lane, at her time of life?

Three hours later, half asleep, bored, cold, and very hungry, he heard the clippertyclop of horse's hooves, the first sign of life since he arrived. As the horse turned the corner into the lane he saw that his ninety five year old Aunt was riding it.

'Good God Auntie, aren't you a bit old to still be riding?'

'You cheeky monkey – who are you anyway?'

'It's George, your nephew, home from the war.'

'Oh, I thought you had been killed' she said – totally indifferent as to whether he had been injured or anything else about his experiences in the war.

'No, a few of us did manage to survive.' He replied sarcastically.

'You'd better come in' she said without any enthusiasm in her voice.

As soon as they had entered the cottage, instead of offering him a cup of tea, which he was gasping for, she launched into an inquisition.

'Why have you come to see me? You never bothered before. Is it my money you are after?' He spluttered. 'NO – well yes – in a way – only a loan though.'

'I thought so. Ancient Aunties who have money are only visited by relatives when they are after their well-earned cash. Sorry, but you are out of luck and have had a wasted journey. As you can see I am as fit as a fiddle. My Mother, your Grandmother, lived to be one hundred and five, and I intend to do the same, so I will need my money to see me through the next ten years and possibly even longer. Do you understand?'

George couldn't believe what he was hearing. The selfish old crone, how dare she talk to him like that? He had been away fighting in a war, being shot at and living under appalling conditions, risking his life for people like her who hadn't even had a bomb dropped nearer than a hundred miles away from their homes. A red mist gathered in front of his eyes and he launched himself at her, knocking her on to the floor.

When the mist cleared, he found himself on top of Millie with his hands around her neck and she was dead, but he had no recollection as to how this had happened.

He had killed many Germans these last few years, so killing was not a new experience for him. 'She deserved it' he told himself by way of an excuse for his murderous action. He went into her kitchen to make himself a cup of tea – the cup she should have had the decency to offer him the minute he walked through her door he thought.. There was a mirror in the kitchen and he caught sight of his face. It was bleeding from scratches on his forehead and cheeks. 'The old girl must have put up a fight' he thought. Bugger, that means I won't be able to go home until they are healed. Mum's bound to question how I got them.' Savouring his tea he thought it doesn't really matter anyway as I need time to set up my alibi before I leave.

He couldn't believe how unaffected he was by his actions. He'd always been a kind caring sort of bloke he thought.

Later, after cooking a delicious meal he prepared from the abundance of ingredients he had found in her kitchen, George lit a fire and settled down to smoke an expensive cigar he found in her sideboard. He poured himself a brandy in a crystal glass that must have cost her as much he earned in a month from his shop. A cigar? She must have a gentleman friend. Laughing, he thought you do have to admire her in some ways. Talk about 'live life to the full'. It seemed age didn't stop his aunt from doing anything. Looking at Millie's corpse lying there on the floor, he quietly contemplated what he needed to do next. Disposing of the body is going to be a problem he thought. Staring into the fire he had lit, he became aware the chimney breast had a recess each side of it. 'Eureka, that's what I'll do; I'll brick up the recesses and bury her behind it, he decided. When he was sitting on the doorstep he had noticed an assortment of building materials stacked up against the side of the cottage. He had thought at the time that maybe she was going to build a garage, as there was certainly the space for one. 'Excellent,' he thought. That means there will be no need to leave the house to go out and buy anything for this project. That's an amazing piece of luck. Earlier when he was waiting for her, he had taken a short walk along the lane to stretch his legs and noticed none of the other cottages appeared to be occupied except number four. It had curtains hanging in the window, but there was no sign of life, so it looked as he wasn't going to have to worry about being observed covering up his crime. 'Must be destiny' he chuckled to himself.

After he had completed the building work, and with auntie safely hidden behind one wall he speculated as to what else he could do to back up the story of her disappearance.

'I know' he said out loud, 'I'll make it look as if she's gone on holiday.'

After making her bedroom look as if she had packed in a hurry, he hid her passport, travelling case, and some holiday type clothes behind the other recess, then bricked that up too.

While he was waiting for the plaster to dry so he could paint the new walls, he took the opportunity to go through her possessions, particularly her paper work to see if he was still her heir. There was a pretty little eighteenth century bureau in her bedroom which looked as if it would be where she would file important papers. It was locked, but with a little gentle persuasion with a nail file, the lock yielded. He found her will amongst other legal papers pertaining to property she owned.

Great, Mum and I are still her beneficiaries, and I was right about the garage.' He found the approval from the local planning department. Then he found a button hidden at the back of the bureau and when he pressed it a drawer shot out full of money – lots of it. 'Eureka, that will solve my immediate cash problems' he shouted, 'and oh what fun I'm going to have when I get my hands on the lot. But I can wait, my plan isn't complete yet. I'll bide my time. My moment will come.'

'Hi Mum, I'm home' he called out.

'I didn't realise you intended to stay with Millie. How did you get on with her?' she replied.

'I never met her Mum. I found her key under a flower pot' he lied, 'so I let myself in and waited nearly a week for her to come back from wherever she had been, then I gave up, and here I am. Did yer' miss me? He said, giving a pat on her bottom.

'Cheeky thing' she laughed.

He looked at his Mother wondering if he had ever loved her, because he felt nothing for her now. He realised he couldn't have done what he did to Millie if he had acted like a normal human being, but he felt he would never be able to act or feel 'normal' again after the trauma he had experienced during the war. He should feel some sort of remorse for murdering his aunt, but he didn't. ' 'Please God, give me back the ability to feel human again,' he prayed to an unresponsive deity.

'Mum I think I'll write to her instead of traipsing all the way down there again, and ask her when it will be convenient for me to call.'

'Good idea son.'

Yes it was he thought. When we finally get around to reporting her missing to the police, they will find my letter, and get in touch with me.

Two months after Aunt Millie's entombment, the Hampshire Police called him.

'A friend of your aunt's was concerned about the lack of communication from her.

Unheard of it appears. She always contacted him at least twice a week without fail he told us. Perhaps you know him? A chap called Roger Prentice.'

'No 'fraid not.' Must have been the man the cigar was purchased for he mused.

'Anyway, he asked us if we could investigate her disappearance. We saw your letters on the doormat when we broke into the cottage, and opened them to see if they gave any indication where she might be. 'Hope you don't mind Sir? Can you throw any further light on the situation?' George had sent this second letter a month after than the first one, to back up his apparent concern about her wellbeing.

'No, that's no problem' he said, hoping he sounded worried. 'But why are you calling? Have you found out where my Aunt might have gone? Would you like me to come down to Daffodil Ridge?'

'That will be very helpful Sir. Ask for me, Inspector Robinson when you get here.'

He arrived at the cottage to find dozens of His Majesties constabulary surrounding the cottage. Then he noticed his aunt's horse grazing in the field just above the ridge. 'Shit, I forgot all about the bloody horse' he thought.

'Good morning Mr Williamson. You look worried.' The Inspector asked, sounding slightly suspicious.

'Sorry' George replied, 'I was looking at my aunt's horse. It wasn't in that field when I was here last.'

'Interesting the inspector commented. Someone must be caring for it. I will have that looked into. Were you very fond of her Mr Williamson?' The inspector asked. He's ex-army George thought, you can always tell so I'll play that card to distract him away from Millie and the bloody horse. How could I have been so sloppy not giving the creature a thought? Who has been looking after it? Should I worry he wondered?

'Yes, I was very fond of her but because I was away fighting for the past five years, unfortunately I hadn't seen her for some time.' The ruse worked.

'Oh I was too. What was your regiment and where did you serve?' Then the two of them got into a lengthy conversation such as ex-soldiers do, and neither Millie nor the horse were mentioned again.

George decided to stay on for a few days, and it turned out to be one of the best decisions of his life, as he met Rose. There was a knock at the door, which sent him into orbit. He opened the door rather hesitantly to be confronted with a vision of loveliness standing on the doorstep. She had shiny blond hair and the bluest of blue eyes, and George was instantly smitten. He had a horrible feeling that he was standing there with his mouth wide open in wonder of this beautiful girl. He hastily rearranged his face and greeted her.

'Er hello – erm - can I help you?'

'Is Mrs Howard in?' the vision asked. 'I've been worried about her as she'd left Delilah without any one to care for her.'

Who the hell is Delilah? Panic; have I missed something? Was this a love child he'd never heard of? This would affect his inheritance?

'Who's Delilah?' he asked casually.

'Her horse, I've been caring for her as nobody else seemed to be.'

He breathed a sigh of relief.

'That was really kind of you. My aunt seems to have disappeared. I'm her nephew George'.

'Disappeared? How very odd. I've called several times to pay her the rent I owe, and wondered where she was. My name is Rose Carter. I live at number four further along the lane.

'Ah, the owner of the curtains, please come in.'

She looked slightly mystified by his remark: then told him she was late with the rent because she had been away for a while to care for her father.

'He had fallen ill, and subsequently died' she told him. Tears rolled down her cheeks and George instinctively gathered her in his arms to comfort her. She laid her head on his chest and sobbed as if it was the most natural thing in the world to do. His body responded to her and a wave of love engulfed him. He had to stop himself from kissing her there and then and he realised she had unlocked feelings him that he thought had gone forever, and he found himself crying with her. Finding that a bit odd she pulled away from him

'Now I know what it feels like to fall in love. I didn't think it would ever happen to me ever again.'

he told her. She looked somewhat bemused and seemed ready to bolt.

'Oh I shouldn't have said that. I'm so sorry. It's just I have felt devoid of feeling anything for anybody -- even my mother -- since the war, and I thought I never would again, until I met you. That's why I was crying.'

In love? That was a bit quick she thought, but nervously gave him a beautiful smile. He decided there and then that he wanted her to be his wife, so in the hope of winning her love he stayed on at the cottage for a while in order for them to get to know each other, completely forgetting Aunt Millie behind the wainscoting.

After a suitable period of time, as nobody had heard from her since she disappeared and because of her great age, it was assumed that Millie had died, possibly on holiday abroad. As Europe was in chaos at the time, with thousands of refugees trying to return to their homeland after the war, the chances of finding an ancient English lady, who may or may not be on holiday there were nil. Therefore the authorities – whoever they might be -

- gave George a death certificate stating Millicent Howard was presumed dead. This enabled him to claim his inheritance without the usual requirement of a body. He grabbed his mother and danced her round the kitchen table singing.

'We're in the money, we're in the money,' he sang lustily -- he was not a gifted vocalist. His mother joined him in the dance, half crying half laughing with tears pouring down her face. Her life had not been easy but now everything was about to change.

Rose and George married almost immediately after the will was read. He because he was madly in love with her, she because she loved him a little, but his new found wealth persuaded her to love him a lot more. He sold the row of cottages on Daffodil Ridge to a property developer Martin Lowe, and the couple moved away to Cornwall, where he bought a magnificent house on the coast for them and their future family and a smaller one nearby for his Mother, who, with his feelings restored, he loved again, and wanted her to be near him.

Rose was very happy – more than she had ever thought she would be in her new life, and loved her husband as much as he loved her. They had three children, a girl and two boys, who George hoped would eventually join him in his very successful travel business. He had encouraged the local Chamber of Commerce to develop tourism in the area thereby helping to turn what had been a beautiful but impoverished village into an equally beautiful, but now prosperous small town. He was due to be Mayor the following year and Rose was busy purchasing suitable clothing for her future role as his Mayoress. A good life, which had been made possible because he had murdered his aunt. An act George seemed to have forgotten.

Oh George! If only your admirers knew the half of it.

No 8 Daffodil Ridge – Part 2

1960

Friends, family, and colleagues, of whom there were many, were gathering for Fergus Reynard's funeral. The Vicar was beginning to worry how on earth they were they all going to fit into his church which he had always thought of as quite large. It was certainly big enough for the dwindling congregation who attended his services these days. What an ungodly lot the English have become he thought to himself, as he smiled through gritted teeth at the throng assembling to pay homage to Fergus, whoever he was, instead of Jesus.

Old friends, who haven't seen each other for a while, would normally rush to greet each other with whoops of joy, but at a funeral ... Oh dear me no! They exchanged banalities:

'Too young to die.'

'Tragic, I can't take it in.'

'She will be devastated.'

'Why was the idiot speeding along that dreadful road?'

And so on in hushed whispers.

Fergus's wife Gillian arrived shrouded in black and propped up by several friends. She was sobbing loudly and continued to do so throughout the service drowning the Vicar's carefully scripted Eulogy. She had decided to have him buried instead of cremated because she wanted him to have a headstone on his grave, so she could visit him every day to talk to him. 'I wouldn't be able to do that if his ashes had been scattered to the four winds would I?' she told her friends.

Gillian had loved her husband, almost to the point of deifying him. In her eyes he was a God, and his sudden death had almost destroyed her. Her best friend Carlotta knew that although Fergus loved his wife dearly, this adoration got on his nerves sometimes.

'I'm just an ordinary bloke' he told her once in a drunken moment. What man can live up to the sort of perfection that she expects from me?'

'Yeah, who indeed?' Carlotta thought.

Fergus had been killed in a car crash. The Police had called on Gillian to give her the terrible news, and WPC Hawks stayed with her until Carlotta arrived to take over from her. PC Johnson, phoned later to give her more details of the crash. Carlotta was pleased she had taken the call as Gillian would have gone into an orbit of despair if she had heard his robotic tones talking about her beloved Fergus in such a bland non emotional way.

'I'm afraid on further examination of the crash site it has been ascertained that Mr Reynard was driving well over the speed limit on the road heading south towards London, when he collided with one of those enormous continental delivery lorries. He didn't have a chance, and would have been killed outright' PC Johnson continued in his monosyllabic tones, and gave details of where Gillian could identify his body.

'Was he heading for London?' Carlotta asked.

'I'm afraid we don't know for certain, but did happen on the main London Road Madam.'

Fergus did a lot of driving to and from building sites for his company as he was their chief architect, but they didn't have any ongoing projects in the south of England, so where was he going that fateful day? Carlotta had met his boss Peter at one of the Reynard's fabulous dinner parties and had flirted with him, so she felt she knew him well enough to approach him at the funeral and ask him if he knew where Fergus was heading that day.

'I've no idea' Peter replied, thrilled to have another chance to talk this exotic looking woman he had met briefly some time ago, when she had roused his dormant libido. .Maybe he could progress his knowledge of her this time, -- a drink one night perhaps.

'Fergus had a couple of days leave owing to him, so he wasn't going to be in the office on Tuesday and Wednesday last week, so wherever he was going, it wasn't work related.' he purred. Carlotta was constantly being 'chatted up' by slavering older men hoping to get into her knickers.

'Interesting, thanks' she said and moved away from a frustrated Peter who had failed to obtain her phone number.

'Day off? Leave? What's Peter talking about. He didn't say anything to ME about any leave.' Gillian sobbed, but the full significance of this didn't hit her until a week after the funeral. Where was he going, and why didn't she know? He always told her everything. -- didn't he? Through her tears at the funeral, she'd noticed a woman holding hands with a little girl about six years old standing by the lynch gate. She thought the child looked vaguely familiar but couldn't quite place her.

'Carlotta, who was that woman with that little girl in the churchyard?' she questioned her friend.

'Who? Oh her. I don't know, 'never seen them before. I wouldn't worry about it. Some people love going to funerals, just like others who go to weddings of people they don't know. They get some weird kick out of it I think. She was probably one of those.'

It was only after all the mourners had finally left her house that Gillian was able to cry unabated, and she did so until there were no more tears left to shed. Later, lying in bed totally drained she gave some thought to the mystery mother and child

Then it struck her, that child looks like Fergus. She had his chestnut hair and big beautiful brown eyes. She was choking; surely it can't be, can it?

Then she thought about Carlotta's reaction to her question as to who they were. Was she imagining things or did she splutter over her reply? Does she know something I don't? Gillian thought. 'No, it simply can't be true' she told herself before she fell into a drugged sleep.

Six months later Gillian was beginning to irritate her friends by constantly droning on about her beloved husband. By now she had elevated him to Valhalla to live with the Gods and it was becoming somewhat tedious. Carlotta couldn't stop herself.

'Come off it Gill, no bloke is that perfect you know. They're all bastards deep down. I wouldn't trust my Leon an inch if he had a chance of bedding some young filly at one of his conferences.'

'How can you say that? I would never doubt Fergus -- ever?'

'Bigger fool you' Carlotta said without thinking – then regretted it.

'What are you getting at?'

Carlotta was flummoxed. How was she going to get herself out of her faux pas?

'I'm not saying he did transgress, just that he had plenty of opportunities if he had wanted to stray with the number of overnight stays he had with his job,' she stammered.

'How dare you make such aspersions about my Felix?' Gillian challenged her friend. Maybe Carlotta was not such a good friend after all slandering him like that she thought.

On her next pilgrimage to the churchyard she saw the mother and child again.

'Why are you standing over my husband's grave?' She demanded.

'It's my Daddy's grave, and I have come to talk to him' the child piped up.

Gillian fainted. When she came to she found the woman bending over her trying to bring her round.

'Get away from me' she yelled and swung her arm out, knocking the woman on the ground. How dare you tell such lies about my husband' she screamed. 'How can he possibly be that child's father? Get off of his grave.'

'I didn't choose to be lying here. You knocked me over remember, and I landed on it.' The woman got to her feet and was surprisingly calm considering she had been assaulted.

'Obviously, I have some explaining to do. By the way my name is Linda and my daughter is Chloe'.

'Chloe! How could he? That was what we were going to call our daughter if we had ever managed to have one. That is too cruel.' Gillian sobbed.

'Oh dear, I'm so sorry. I'm afraid I didn't know that'.

'How could he have deceived me so?'

More sobbing this time accompanied by Chloe, who was totally confused by the adult's behaviour? Grownups are very strange she thought, and decided there and then that she wasn't going to be one and would stay as a child forever.

'There's a cafe in the church. I think it might be a good idea if we go in and have a cup of coffee and talk things over.' Linda suggested. Gillian didn't answer, but allowed herself to be steered .towards the church. In the cafe Linda apologised to her and told her she was never meant to find out about Chloe'.

'Where do you live' Gill demanded.

'Ealing -- in London'.

'So was he coming to see you the day he died?

'I'm afraid so, although it wasn't me so much as Chloe he wanted to see. Our affair, -- well you really couldn't call it that was only going to be a bit of fun but I got pregnant and Fergus begged me to keep the baby.'

'Where did you meet? Gill asked through gritted teeth, not really wanting to know and destroy what was left of the memories of her husband.

'Fergus's firm had designed a new headquarters for the company I worked for and I met him on the building site. I promise you it was not some grand passion; he loved you too much to ever leave you. It was just a bit of fun' she repeated rather sheepishly. 'He told me how much you both wanted to have children and that it just wasn't happening for you, so he couldn't bring himself to allow me to murder his first child in case he never had another one. He said he had a good job and promised me he would always support Chloe, even if you two managed to conceive eventually. He even offered to make a legal declaration to confirm the fact he was Chloe's father, but I told him that wasn't necessary.

Well as I was getting on a bit, -- nearly thirty, and as there was nobody I was dating that I thought was husband material, plus I had always intended to have children, I thought why not?'

'How can you be so cold and calculating over something as important as a child's future?'

'Yeah it doesn't sound too good saying it out loud to his wife does it? Sorry about that, but as I told you it wasn't a love affair, and frankly I'm surprised he hadn't had the odd dalliance before. Most of them do you know'.

'What do you mean accusing ALL men? You're shameful, do you know that?

'That's not the first time I've been told that.' Linda replied, grinning.

Gillian was shocked. 'You have no shame. We have nothing more to say to each other.' As they parted, Linda thrust her telephone number at Gill, saying if she ever wanted to speak to her again— even if it was just to scream at her, ' please don't hesitate to call'.

'That's not going to happen – EVER' she answered, but she kept the phone number nevertheless.

As soon as she arrived home she phoned Carlotta'

'You knew didn't you, you evil witch?'

'Knew? Knew what? Oh shit, you've found out. I'm coming over.'

'Don't bother. I never want to see you ever again.'

'Too bad, I'm on my way.'

It transpired one or two of Gillian's friends knew he was either in, or had had some kind of relationship outside of his marriage. He had been seen with a dark haired woman a couple of times in a pub just off the motorway.

'Yes, that sounds like Linda, she has dark hair. Unless it was some other floozy he had tucked away in his murky past.'

'Come off it Gillian: you know that's not true.' Carlotta mumbled, trying to soften the blow a bit but Gillian felt utterly betrayed and a complete fool.

Whatever must I have sounded like to my friends when I constantly sang his praise when they knew differently about what I thought was my saintly husband' she thought. The embarrassment was too much for her to bear and she decided there and then she was leaving the Chalfonts, and moving as far away as she possibly could from this place.

She couldn't live with the humiliation and shame of everybody laughing at her, knowing her life had been a lie. She rushed away, yelling at her friend as she went.

'I never want to see you or any of my so called friends EVER again, and DON'T try to find me. '

I'm not sure I want to when you're behaving like this' Carlotta thought. But she felt sorry for her friend and wished she could help her in some way.

Selling her house was easy, situated where it was in the commuter belt, but knowing where to move to was a difficult decision to make. Her first choice had been either the Isles of Scilly or the Shetlands, the furthest places she could think of away from her treacherous friends, but on reflection, she felt maybe that was a bit excessive and settled for an isolated terrace of cottages in Hampshire called Daffodil Ridge, and chose the one at the end of the cul-de-sac with only one immediate neighbour.

Martin Lowe, the developer who purchased Daffodil Ridge from George Williamson, had discovered some time later that he wasn't going to be able to knock the cottages down and build houses in the area as he had anticipated as they were over two hundred years old and Grade 2 listed, therefore protected by law from being demolished. At first he was furious, and threatened to take George to court for not telling him. This was the mildest of his threats, the rest were far more bloodthirsty. However, in the fullness of time the charm and history of these ancient homes began to grow on him, and he decided he would restore them and then sell them individually to the burgeoning middle class earth mother types who were beginning to pop up all over the place wearing homespun and talking in genteel voices about 'returning to their roots'. However, they didn't want their 'roots' not to include twenty first century bathrooms, so he applied for planning permission to build at the back of the cottages to extend the footprint of the buildings and give him the extra space to build the bathrooms. After he was rejected a couple of times, he threatened the Conservation Department of the local council, that if they continued to refuse him he would let the cottages fall into disrepair to the point where they would fall down of their own accord. He pointed out his plans didn't change the outward look of the cottages so eventually, after countless committee meetings common sense prevailed, and he got his permission.

A good ten years had passed since then, and Gillian thought the cottages were beginning to look a bit shabby so she set about restyling her new home for something to do and busied herself searching for period wall papers and the correct colour paints for the cottage. Now it was finished she found herself lonely, unoccupied and bored, and she rather wished she hadn't been so off hand and dismissive of her neighbour, who had offered the hand of friendship on more than one occasion. Also the silence which she thought she had craved was beginning to get her down, and what was that scratching noise from behind the wainscoting? Even if it was only mice it was unnerving. She was beginning to regret cutting off all connections with her old friends. 'Shall I ring Carlotta?' she thought. 'But maybe she won't want to speak to me. I was pretty horrible to her when I left and I didn't even say goodbye. I do miss her' she thought and her tears started to flow – again! 'I don't think I handled Fergus's death very well, and I don't know how to rectify the situation' she mused.

Two weeks later she found a letter on her mat. It was an invitation to a party from her neighbour Anne- Marie. The invitation said – 'Although she appreciated she had made it perfectly clear she didn't want to have anything to do with any of her neighbours, it was going to be a very noisy party and would spill over into the lane and she might find it more pleasant to attend, rather than sit in her house with a racket going on until late – very late'. Gillian decided this was an opportunity to make amends and decided to call on Anne- Marie and apologise. She was shaking as she knocked on her door.

'Oh -- Hi. Thank you for your invitation. I would love to come to the party', she gabbled nervously. 'And I'm sorry I was so offhand with you before.' she added.

Anne – Marie looked surprised, then smiled and invited her in for coffee.

Gillian found herself opening up to her neighbour, telling her about Fergus's infidelity and what she saw as her friends betrayal as her reason for moving away from the Chalfonts.

'I felt let down by him and my so called friends. That's why I've become so reclusive' she explained. Anne-Marie was sympathetic but critical at the same time.

'Silly cow, why did you get yourself in such a state over a bloke, even if you did love him? Gillian was a bit shocked at her talking to her so bluntly when she had only just met her, but said nothing. The pleasure of actually speaking to a real person outweighed any criticism she may have felt towards Anne-Marie's out spoken manner. Maybe she was right anyway she thought

'You remind me of my friend Carlotta.' she said 'She says what she thinks like you.' Anne-Marie changed the subject, being somewhat bored with Gillian's tale of woe.

'By the way Gilly, do you ever hear funny noises from our joining wall?'

She wasn't keen on being called Gill, much preferring Gillian, but was so happy just talking to someone that she didn't correct her new friend.

'What, a sort of scratching?' she asked surprised. 'I presumed it was mice and put some traps down but I've never managed to catch any.'

'Yeah, a bit like that, only I do, and Mrs Mortimer who lived there before you often heard scratching noises. I find it a bit creepy but it's probably only my imagination playing tricks ... Old houses always creak don't they?' She paused. 'Hey, I've got an idea. There's a fete in the village this week- end and I'm organising it. Why don't you give me a hand to run one of the stalls? It'll give you a chance to meet some of the other Daffodils before the party.' Anne-Marie said.

'Daffodils? What do you mean?'

Anne- Marie shrieked with laughter. 'Sorry, the residents of Daffodil Ridge, that's what we call ourselves'. Gillian had never been keen on community functions -- all that collecting of other peoples rubbish, only to have to get rid of it when it didn't sell was how she saw jumble sales, but felt she was obliged to say yes to make up for her previous rudeness.

The whole village took part setting up the site with bunting and brightly coloured cloths to cover the makeshift tables. People brought out cakes, bric-a-brac, and all manner of items good, bad and indifferent, and some only fit for the dustbin, to sell to make money for their chosen charity. Terry Whittaker from number two the Ridge was very much in evidence helping to lift all the heavy stuff and joking with the other volunteers. There was always laughter wherever he was. Anne- Marie caught Gill looking at him.

'Now he's a catch darling. Divorced about three years ago, probably ready for a serious relationship by now, plus he's got a good job and he's not bad looking either. Go for it.' she encouraged Gillian.

'Oh no, I'm not looking for a relationship right now' she stuttered, blushing as she protested. Later she asked herself, do I want to spend the rest of my life being the not so merry widow? NO I don't. Fergus is dead but I'm not, and he deceived me, so why should I remain true to him? So she gave Terry a beguiling smile. He came across to their stall.

Anne-Marie chuckled. 'Are you sure you don't want a 'feller?' she asked.

'Hi, I'm Terry from number two.. I've seen you passing my house. It's lovely to meet you at last.'

The day of the party arrived. It was a beautiful day and all the residents of Daffodil Ridge were in and out of each other's houses carrying food and drink and loading it onto a long table they had erected in the lane as the weather forecast was so good. Gillian opened up her house along with the rest of the residents, and spoke to many of them apologising for being so off hand and unfriendly with them before.

'My husband died' she told them 'and I am afraid I took it very badly'

Terry was never very far from her side, and she could see the envy in one or two of the 'Daffodil's' eyes. The wine flowed and it was a fantastic party, and at the end of it, much to her surprise she found herself in Terry's bed. And so her new life began.

Everything was going well for her and she was filled with joy with her new found love. She decided to write to her old friend Carlotta, to apologise for her dismissal of her last time they met, and to tell her of her new relationship.

'I'm too much of a coward to phone her as she might hang up on me as I was such a bitch the last time we met.' she told Anne-Marie. Carlotta did respond of course, and came down to see Gillian in her new home as soon as she was able.

'This place is pretty but a bit spooky isn't it? But then it's old, and dozens of people must have lived here. All manner of things could have happened over the years to leave their imprint.' Carlotta commented.

'Do you think so? I can't say I have noticed an atmosphere – only that scratching noise from behind that wall.' Gillian told her friend.

'Ooh! — That could be a spirit trying --- '

'Stop scaring me'. Gill interrupted her. 'It's probably mice.'

Their relationship now firmly established Terry stayed at number eight far more frequently than his own cottage. Then one night Gill sat bolt upright in bed.

'Who was that speaking?' she called out.

A quavering voice repeated, 'Call her Millie. Get the bastard. Call her Millie.'

'Whatever is the matter darling? You are as white as a sheet.' Terry said.

'There was a voice as clear as yours telling me something, but I can't think what she said.'

'Oh it was a she then' Terry laughed.'

38

'Definitely, it was something like 'call her Millie.'

Two months later, much to her surprise she discovered she was pregnant.

'That's odd' she told Terry. 'I thought I couldn't have children.'

So delighted at the news, they hurriedly arranged a wedding to take place in a month's time. The very long guest list was compiled of friends from her previous life and her new ones post Fergus. Terry was not exactly short of friends and relations either, so they were added to the already long list. Carlotta and Anne-Marie were to act as her Maids of Honour. When they met they got on famously as Gillian knew they would, and got very drunk together at the reception. It was a grand affair in an expensive hotel and was thoroughly enjoyed by everyone. Six months later, a seven pound six ounces baby girl made her entry into the world. Without thinking why, they named her Millie.

'What would you reaction be if I suggested moving to France? Terry asked her one morning. 'There's an advert for a vineyard for sale here in the Sunday Times.'

'What do we know about running a vineyard?' She protested.

'Might be fun.' He responded.

'Yeah, Why not?' Her response surprised her conservative self.

'Wow,' Terry exclaimed. 'I didn't expect you to agree so quickly. Fantastic!'

And so the nearly new, newlyweds, decided to up sticks and move to France for a completely new life. They sold both their cottages and bought the vineyard at a knock down price. A brave -- or maybe foolhardy move -- as their only experience of wine was drinking it, -- lots of it.

As she was packing and sorting out her belongings, Gill came across a collection of Fergus's architectural drawings. She was about to throw them away when it flashed across her mind that his daughter might want them. This came as a great surprise to her to think of Chloe as his daughter.

'I'm about to embark on a new life in a new country, with a new, well newish husband and a new baby, so maybe I'll give Linda a ring.' she told Anne-Marie 'and pass on some of Fergus's stuff to her.'

'Sorry, who's that?-- Gillian? – Oh Gillian Reynard. Hi'.

'Yes. But I have remarried and I'm Gillian Whittaker now, and I am viewing the world in a different way as a result, and I was wondering if Chloe would like some of her father's architectural drawings?' Taken aback Linda didn't reply for a while.

'She – I would be delighted. It's really very generous of you. Thank you so much.'

'I've got some of his books too, and some photographs of him as a child I could give you those as well' She felt slightly guilty getting rid of her memories of Fergus, only keeping a few bits and pieces, but she felt every child had the right to know their father was, even illegitimate ones like Chloe. After all they didn't ask to be born. Gillian also found pictures of his long dead parents. They died of a fever in India long before she met Fergus, so she put those in the box she had made up for the girl. She still had trouble saying Chloe. Chloe was to be the name of Fergus and her unborn daughter, not Linda's, and she still felt a sadness that they hadn't had children before his untimely death.

The meeting took place and Gillian seeing Linda in these different circumstances, could understand why Fergus had been attracted to her. She was good fun, intelligent and a positive person. She wouldn't have been so negative if her husband had died the way she had. Linda would have mourned him sincerely and then moved on, not spending her life weeping and wailing and eventually sanctifying him. There's a lesson here I must learn she thought.

Linda was over the moon receiving so many items for Chloe to have of her father's, and was really grateful to Gillian for giving them to her.

'I've always felt worried that when Chloe was older she would want to know more about her father's life, and might judge me harshly for sleeping with a married man I barely knew. But because of your generosity and forgiveness, she will know some of his background and that puts my affair on a different level.' Linda said.

Gillian feeling magnanimous adjusted her halo as she waved her goodbye.

After a rocky start, France proved to be a successful move for the three of them and a brother and sister eventually arrived to join Millie in their French idyll.

Did George's Aunt Millie know her namesake had become a little French girl?

Only a psychic would know the answer to that question.

No 8 Daffodil Ridge - Part 3

1968

When Maureen McAllister was seventeen, her ambition was to be a hippie. Not that she had any idea what a hippie's ethos or lifestyle was really like , but she loved the brightly coloured and scruffy clothes they wore, and they seemed to do as they liked. They roamed around the country: lived in tepees and listened to her sort of music. An idyllic life; unlike her present one.

Her parents were members of a particularly strict non-conformist church and the only music allowed in their house were requiems and hymns. Her reading material was also censored. She felt she was a prisoner in her parents' home, and couldn't wait to get away.

Now she knew differently, but at one time had been convinced the stork had dropped her down the wrong chimney. The only reason she now knew the truth was because a school friend of hers had enlightened her to the true facts, where storks and chimneys didn't feature, but parts of the male body did. The friend told her what men did with one particular member in order to produce babies. Maureen had great difficulty in believing this to be true and began to look at her brothers in a different light. Would they really have to do that when they wanted a family? Did her Dad do it - THREE TIMES? She was horrified.

Un-ironed clothes were one of the many cardinal sins, of which there were many in her parents, 'God's book of unacceptable behaviour.' But she was the one who had to iron everybody's clothes, jeans, tee shirts, and sweaters and she HATED it. . Hippies didn't look as if they knew what an iron was, which was another reason for wanting to join them. She resolved once she had left home she would never ever iron another piece of clothing again.

'Did God give this book to Moses on Mount Sinai along with the Ten Commandments?' Maureen asked her Mother in all innocence, and received a swipe round her legs with a wet dish cloth for being cheeky

She worked in the Paradise Coffee Bar in the High Street which belonged to one of her parent's church friends. They would only permit her to work in a place where one of the brethren could keep a watchful eye on her to make sure she didn't mix with the wrong type of people. That meant anyone who wasn't a member of their peculiar religious sect. Non-believers were not encouraged to enter the cafe, so business was not exactly brisk.

Maureen wanted to experience how ordinary people lived without all these ghastly restrictions being imposed on her, and her resolve to escape deepened.

She was supposed to give her Mother the money she earned at the cafe towards her keep, but this week she rebelled. She bought herself a long Indian multi coloured skirt and a purple top out of her tips as the first items in her hippie wardrobe. She tried to sidle past her parents when she arrived home, and crept upstairs hoping they wouldn't notice her. No chance there!

'Where do you think you are going young lady?'

Oh bugger, they've got eyes in the back of their heads, she thought. This was a word she had picked up at school and she was amazed the first time she uttered it that hell fire and brimstone didn't descend from the heavens to swallow her up, as she had been told it would. She spluttered, -- 'I've got a headache and I was going straight to bed.'

'Where's your money. Were you going to keep it to buy alcohol?'

Idiots she thought. 'How on earth can I buy any form of booze when I'm under age? They're obsessed.'

'No Mum ... I'm ... 'erm' then she gabbled,' I was robbed on the way home.'

'Liar' her parents said in unison, and sent her to her room to learn passages of the Bible as a punishment. This happened frequently as whatever she did it was wrong according to her parents who thought she was the spawn of the Devil. But not so her brothers, who her Mother believed had descended from the Angels. This was so unfair that she decided today was the day she would make her escape.

She packed her Post Office savings book, her new skirt and top, and a few other bits and pieces and climbed out of her bedroom window, a skill she had perfected over the past couple of months, unbeknown to her parents. They naively thought locking her into her room at night would keep her safe from the sinful world outside where rapists and non-believers lived.

The next bit could be tricky. She had to slide down the sloping roof over the scullery of the small Victorian house they lived in and then jump down into the garden and make a mad dash to the back gate without being noticed. Once she arrived in the alleyway at the back of the house, she was free to meet her new friends at the Copacabana which she had been doing in secret once a week ever since she learnt how to escape the confines of her room.

She made for the cafe where they hung out and by a stroke of luck, Nick was there surrounded by his cronies as usual. He was a good friend to her and recognising her vulnerability he strangely felt the need to protect her. In the days when he lived in his family home, he looked out for his five younger sisters, so taking care of young girls became second nature to him. He was a good looking lad, nearly six foot tall, with a mop of dark curly hair and big brown eyes. The girls in the cafe all drooled over him, but Maureen seemed unaware of this. She just saw him as her mate. Nick's posse couldn't understand why he bothered with Maureen at all. She was nothing to look at, neither plain nor pretty and her hair was lank and mousey. Her eyes were a pretty shade of blue, spoilt by being rather bulbous.

'Nick, where do you think I could join up with a band of hippies?' She asked him.

He looked at her in amazement.

'Are you serious?

'Yes, I've left home, and that's what I want to do – live in a commune.'

'What brought this on? He asked her somewhat mystified. 'Sorry 'luv', no idea where hippies hang out'. She looked defeated; he paused.

'Oh, hang on a 'mo. I think there's a massive gathering outside the American Embassy protesting about the Vietnam War, and there's another one 'Banning the Bomb' somewhere -- 'can't remember where, but I'm pretty sure there's a load of them taking part in both of these protests up west. What happened to make you suddenly leave home anyway?'

'I can't live by their weird rules a moment longer. Since I've known you lot I've realised it's not normal the way they interpret God's word.' The gang looked confused. Who was this God person? He didn't have anything to do with them.

She didn't give Nick a chance to persuade her to go home and piped up 'How do I get to the Embassy?'

'It's in Grosvenor Square. Listen, I know you have a hard time at home, but you're not really equipped to make it on your own. You've had no experience of the big wide world, and it can be pretty rough out there.' She looked crestfallen.

Nick looked at her sad face. 'Oh 'gawd! You won't have a clue how to negotiate the tube but if you're so determined, I think I had better come with you to find them, 'cos you're a bit young to go wandering off on your own.'

'I'm eighteen next month.' she stated indignantly.

'Love, that's as maybe numerically, but you're much younger mentally. You've got a lot of catching up to do.' In her heart she knew he was right, so she didn't argue with him.

When they arrived at the Embassy, they mingled with a group of protesting hippies handing out flowers and with placards stating 'MAKE LOVE, NOT WAR'. Nick was hoping he could to get into conversation with them later when the square cleared a bit to find out where they hung out. There was a very pretty girl with flowers in her hair he thought was highly 'fanciable, so he sidled up to her.

'Hi I'm Nick. Where are you lot going after the protest?' She looked startled.

'What do you mean, you lot? We're going home.' She said indignantly.

'Where's that?' he asked

'Wherever we lay our heads' she responded dreamily.

What sort of daft answer is that he mused, but he was on a mission for his friend so he persisted.

'My friend Maureen wants to join you.'

'Ask Oberon, he's sort of our Leader --- Well, he's not really as we are all free spirits, but he is the most practical one in our commune, and he takes charge when we leave it.' Nick went across to meet up with the non-leader.

'Hi I'm Nick.'

'Peace love and happiness be with you man.'

What a prize twit, Nick thought. I can't leave Maureen alone with this load of screwballs.

I suppose I had better go with her for a bit. She'll soon get tired of them and then we can come back home.

'My friend and I were looking to join a commune.'

'We would be happy to absorb you into our way of life and ideology if you are serious and prepared to share the work load: give up material things, and commune with nature along with your fellow man. If that's what you are seeking, then we would be happy for you to join us.' What has she got me into Nick thought, but hey ho, why not give it a try I haven't got much else going for me at the moment.

'Thank you, I'll just go and get my friend and we will follow you.'

'We've got room on the bus if you are serious, follow Saffron'.

'Which one's Saffron?'

'The girl you were talking to earlier.'

He collected Maureen telling her they were going to go back to their commune with them. She's so flipping unworldly, maybe this spaced out lot could be right for her Nick mused.

'Are you coming with me? Say yes. It will be such fun.' she pleaded.

'Dunno about that. Maybe I'll stay a couple of weeks, just to see you settle in.'

At that point the once peaceful protest erupted into full scale war. The ten thousand protesters had originally gathered in Trafalgar Square where the actress Vanessa Redgrave, had addressed the crowd on the evils of the nuclear bomb, then hundreds of protesters marched on to Grosvenor Square to continue their protest outside the American Embassy. That was when the trouble started. There was a police cordon around the grounds which the protesters had managed to break through and they swarmed across the lawns right up to the entrance of the building. This cumulated with a protracted battle between the agitators and the police, where dozens from both groups were injured, some seriously. When the mounted officers began to charge into the crowd on their huge horses, Nick decided enough was enough, -- he was off. He managed to find Maureen who was looking terrified and dragged her through the crowd collecting Saffron along the way. He left the two girls sitting on the pavement sobbing, forbidding them to move an inch until he returned, and went back o find Oberon and his not so merry men and girls. Violence was not part of their doctrine, so they had no idea how to deal with it when they found themselves in the middle of a battle. Nick rallied them and finally a subdued group reassembled by the bus Oberon had hired to take them to and from the protest and headed off back to their commune about one hundred and twenty miles away from London. Nick looked at the vehicle, which was definitely on its last legs and speculated on how far they would get before it died. He underestimated the time, as they had barely left central London before it gasped, coughed, and spat out a lot of smoke then shuddered to a halt. The hippies all stood around looking at it in its death throes, but nobody made any attempt to do anything to resolve the situation. Oberon's so called practical side failed to reveal itself, as he was staring at the dying beast along with the rest of his group.

Nick was man of many talents and repairing engines was one of them.

He found endless pleasure from a very young age dismantling anything mechanical or electrical and reassembling it. However he had never applied these skills into actually getting paid employment which was a total anathema to him. He preferred to take money from the government in order to survive instead of working by deliberately failing every interview he was sent to by the Job Centre. They eventually came to the conclusion he was a halfwit who would never be able to hold down a job, and decided it would be much easier just to give him his money every week without question. This was far from the truth, as he was highly intelligent and could have joined MENSA if he felt so inclined, except he never did.

Nicks skills were needed now as never before -- much to his annoyance, as he never wanting to be in charge of anything, but he felt unless he took control of this situation, they would all be standing here staring at the bus for eternity. Having assessed the damage he decided it was possible to make a temporary repair, but the long term prognosis was certain death. He sent several of the hairy men off to find a garage to buy various bits and pieces for him with which they miraculously managed to achieve. Nick against all the odds, got the terminally ill beast going, hoping it would survive long enough to get them to wherever home was. On the road, Oberon thanked him profusely.

'You will be a valuable asset to our community' he exclaimed.

'What did you do for a living before you took up your present life style?' Nick queried.

'I was, and am, a poet.'

'That wouldn't bring the pennies in mate, so how do you manage financially? What did the rest of the group do before they joined?'

'Well, let me think. Pease Blossom was a nurse, Judas was a priest and ...'

Nick burst out laughing interrupting him.

'Was this before or after he earned his thirty pieces of silver?'

'If you are going to mock us, its best you leave us right now.' Oberon said sulkily.

'Then what will you do when this load of crap breaks down again, because I can assure you it will.' Oberon went quiet, and then later feigned sleep in order to avoid speaking to Nick. They continued on their journey until the next break down, and then – inevitably the next one, where Nick surprised himself by managing to get the bus moving yet again, even if it was only in second gear.

'You can thank whoever your God is that we haven't encountered many traffic lights in the last fifty miles, or we would never have made it' he told them when they finally arrived at their site.

---.

Life in the commune was gentle, peaceful, and going nowhere. They grew their own food, shared the tasks such as cooking, cleaning, looking after the chickens etc. This was a vegetarian group much to Nick's disgust being a great lover of meat in all its forms. They ate the eggs, but the chickens were allowed to wander around even when they had stopped laying, eventually dying of old age. The group perfected various crafts, and sold them at local markets to raise money for any expenses they incurred. Skye had become adept at making jewellery with seeds and other organic matter she could dye and utilise. This life was fine if you lacked ambition, but irritating if you thought you were stagnating as Nick did. He and Maureen now renamed Skye, were sharing a tepee, and one or two occasional lovers, which was part of the lifestyle in the commune. Getting off their heads on weed, having sex whenever they felt like it, and singing protest songs around a camp fire in the evenings was great -- for a while, but the slow pace of the lifestyle eventually began to pall for Nick.

Skye was pregnant and in spite of their sexual freedom, he knew it to be his, and he wanted to move on, but not having much of an idea as to where. He knew if he left Maureen, (he couldn't get his head around calling her Skye) with the commune, she and her baby would be cared for, but did he want his son or daughter to live this negative life? No, he didn't think so, which meant he would have to take her with him. Mm-m, a quandary? He had never felt the need to do something with his life before, but now he did, but still had no idea how to change things or what he actually wanted to do, but leave he must?

'Sorry to see you go. If you change your mind we will be delighted to have you back with us again.' Oberon said. I bet you would Nick thought. It's me who runs this set up, and thinks ahead as to what we should do and how we can raise money for necessities. Some leader you turned out to be he thought.

'You never know mate. I may see the error of my ways and return to the fold'

Nick said sarcastically.

So they packed their bags and left. Skye loved her hippie name and and living in the commune and didn't want to leave but couldn't envisage life without Nick so she trailed after him sobbing. They wandered from town to town like gypsies, taking work wherever they could find it. Skye used her jewellery making skills, selling items in local markets and Nick turned his hand to anything from gardening: repairing cars, or working in burger bars to make a little money. They drifted along without making any real changes to their lives and Nick was beginning to get despondent, as he was no nearer to knowing what he wanted to do now than when he was in the commune. They eventually returned to the suburbs of London, where they managed to rent a flat just before Maureen gave birth to Jake. For the first time since she left home she wondered if she should contact her parents and let them know they were now grandparents, but rejected the idea immediately. They would only call him a bastard, and want to take him away from her to bring him up in the true ways of their peculiar God.

Jake was a beauty; he had his father's brown eyes and his mother's laid back temperament, and was a very easy child to look after, and before long, she was pregnant again. This time they had a little girl who they called Leila. Now Nick felt well and truly trapped. This wasn't what he left the commune for, but with the added encumbrance of two children... his kids ... and he loved them, so he couldn't bring himself to just up and leave, so what could he do? The flat was far too small for the four of them, so Nick approached the council to re-house them.

'No chance there' the housing officer informed him. 'Properties in London are at a premium.'

'We don't need to stay in London.'

'Ah well, that's a different story. Maybe I can help you.'

He made a couple of phone calls to other authorities.

'Do you mind living in a pretty but remote area in Hampshire?' he asked hopefully.

'That'll do fine.' said Nick 'If you can you give us the fare to get there?'

'Yeah, no problem. It'll get you off our books, and release your present flat for some other desperate soul who needs to live in London.'

And so Skye and Nick and their two kids found themselves in a rundown cottage in Daffodil Ridge. She loved it, he hated it.

Daffodil Ridge had undergone dramatic changes over the years and cute cottages, once desired by the 'back to nature' middle class environmentalists' who abounded in the sixties and seventies no longer existed, and the pendulum had swung in the opposite direction. Small was no longer beautiful, and now the 'must have' properties the middle classes were large Victorian houses in urban green areas. They wanted somewhere to accommodate their families where they could knock down walls and rearrange the interiors the way they wanted a massive kitchen living area being an absolutely essential, also a drawing room, a study, a play room, and en suite bathrooms in every bedroom. All of this without bringing the conservation police out in full force. They also needed to be within easy access to London, where the bread winner of the family, male or female could earn the high salaries and huge bonuses required in order to finance these expensive monoliths.

The cottages on Daffodil Ridge failed to fill any of these requirements and gradually slipped into decline. The once proud owners of their Grade 2 conservation buildings, if they wanted to relocate, had to sell them at a knock down price to the local council who were desperately in need of properties to house their ever increasing housing list. So when Nick and Maureen – sorry Skye -- moved in to number eight, apart from Anne- Marie in number seven and Brenda in number three the rest of the occupants were all council tenants, re-housed from the big cities and unfamiliar with country life. Daffodils now longer bloomed in a blaze of golden yellow to herald the coming of Spring as they once had all along the ridge. They had been destroyed by the multitude of kids now living in the cottages, constantly clambering over them to get to the field beyond to play football, leaving the bulbs and earth scattered in their wake. The two or three children of the previous owners would never have dreamt of doing such a thing if their parents forbade it. They would walk round the back of the cottages and along the lane to the gate leading to the field. The new kids had a leader, Tom a big lad from number six who led his army in a war like attack over the bank to the field beyond with destruction following in their wake.

There was a knock on Skye's door.

'Hi, I'm your neighbour Anne- Marie Mason' she said, and gave Skye a homemade cake as a welcome present. From her hippie days, she was aware of the value people of Anne-Marie's class put on 'homemade' and was duly grateful, although she actually preferred shop bought herself. Anne-Marie was a tall a striking looking brunette, not pretty but attractive in a dramatic way, probably in her mid to late fifties, but very friendly.

'Come in' Skye invited her, 'I haven't settled in yet but I am sure I can rustle up a cup of tea. Nick's off looking for work.'

'Is Nick your husband?'

'Sort of' she replied somewhat embarrassed.

'Please don't worry about tea, but I will just pop in for a chat, if I'm not holding you up with your unpacking'. Skye, didn't like to say she had finished, and what Anne-Marie could see was all they owned, possessions being frowned upon in the hippie world, and an encumbrance when they were wandering around the country.

'How long have you lived here?' Skye asked her neighbour.

'It feels like I've never lived anywhere else, which is not true, but it's actually thirty years plus' she told her. 'I've seen so many people come and go from here that it gets depressing.' Wondering why she moved here in the first place if she disliked it so much Skye asked her if she had ever considered leaving.

'A thousand times, but no bugger wants to live in this God forsaken neck of the woods now, and we would lose so much money by selling up, that we wouldn't be able to buy anywhere in a half decent area with the money we would get, so we are stuck here. Incidentally have you heard a scratching noise from the wainscoting yet?'

'Yes I have, I presumed it was mice, but I haven't seen any.'

'No you won't. We have never been able to work out what causes it. Anyway, I'll let you get on, and you must come for a cup of tea with me very soon.'

'Thanks', I will.'

As Skye opened her door to let her neighbour out, her children burst in the door, shouting at the top of their voices about a kid who had committed some crime or other against them.

'Mum, they called us gypsies.'

'Stop yelling for goodness sake.' Skye ordered. She didn't want her neighbour thinking they were common, even if they were.

'Great to meet you kids. What are your names and how old are you both? Ann-Marie asked. They spoke in unison, drowning each other out.

'Oh for goodness sake the pair of you, answer properly.' Skye embarrassed by their behaviour ordered. The change was dramatic. Jake told her his name and that he was eight years old, and Leila, speaking beautifully for once, said that she was six and a half.

Anne-Marie was impressed.

Time passed at its usual rapid way and in what seemed like a mere six months, two years had rushed by. Nick and Skye realised that unbelievably they had been together for twelve years.

'Maureen, sit down. I need to speak to you about the future', Nick said.

She was worried about the way he spoke as it sounded serious. He had been very restless ever since they had moved into Daffodil Ridge and she was scared that he wanted to leave her. How on earth am I going to manage if he does? I will never be able to cope on my own she thought to herself, and sat down warily to hear what he had to say.

'We've been together a long time now love, but you and I both know that was never how our relationship was meant to be. We were never in love were we? I only went along with you to set you up with a bunch of hippies, and then I was going to go back home, but somehow that time has stretched on for twelve years, and I really have to leave now or I will go insane. I need to find myself – I know that sounds crass, but I really do. I'm thirty two years old and for too long I have been drifting along living your life, but now it's my turn.

I will always support the kids as far as I possibly can. It might be that I will send little money one week, a lot more another, and next to nothing the following, depending what I earn, but I won't desert my responsibilities to you or our kids I promise you that.' Skye was rooted to her chair, and stared at him goggle eyed, saying nothing. It unnerved him, but he carried on.

'It's not only for my sake, but yours as well, because you've hardy developed at all in all these years as you've just drifted along changing nothing. At the commune here were hundreds of books.'

'Yes I remember, you always had your nose stuck in one 'she interrupted him.

'I was learning all the time, but you've just remained the way you'd always been, and haven't changed a bit in twelve years. There were many opportunities to develop in the commune. There were many educated people there who would have been only too pleased to pass on their knowledge to anyone who was interested, but you never took advantage of this opportunity. Without me to rely on maybe you will grow as an individual. You could expand your artistic skills. Take a course, learn how to market your work, but please do something with your life. This place is great for you and the kids. The people are friendly, and there are children our two can play with. Go to the council and tell them I've left you and tell them to put the cottage in your name. A few tears may help you get some benefits. Right I'm afraid that's it love, I'm off. I'll be in touch' and with that he was gone leaving Skye in floods of tears and with a broken heart she thought would never mend.

Six months later.

Well it did mend. Nick was right; she had relied on him for everything and now felt ashamed of herself for doing so. She missed him desperately as he had been a part of her life for so long. True to his word, he did send her money on a 'regular irregular' sort of way. He kept in touch with the kids by sending them postcards of different towns when he was travelling then letters once he settled in York. Much to her surprise Skye found she could manage on her own quite well. Not that she liked doing it, but she had succeeding in getting the cottage in her name, sorted out her benefits, and with Anne-Marie's help by babysitting, she had started an Art course at the college which included jewellery making along with pottery, drawing, and other skills. She loved it, and was angry with herself for not having done something similar years ago. As Nick had said to her, she'd had plenty of opportunities in the commune.

'Hi, I've brought someone to meet you.' It was Anne-Marie with Brenda from number three.

'Hi. Nice to meet you' Skye greeted Brenda. 'I've seen you about, but we have never met before, do come in. Would you like tea or coffee or maybe a fruit juice?' Skye fussed about getting cups and saucers out for her visitors. She and Anne-Marie always used mugs, but she had a feeling there was something different about today so she made a bit of an effort.

'You can feel something here can't you Bren?' Anne-Marie prompted her.

'Yes, there's definitely a presence here'.

'You're frightening me; what do you mean a presence?' Skye asked alarmed.

'Something bad happened here.' Brenda pronounced. As well as being a medium, she was a full time dinner lady at the local school. Skye couldn't quite get her head around the two personas. Who ever heard of a medium called

Brenda? She should be Madam something or other she thought.

'It's inevitable something bad has happened here,' Anne Marie piped up. 'These places are at least two hundred and fifty years old so it's unlikely it was always a happy home. The ancients lived through war, plague and famine and heaven knows what else, so . . .

'No no,' Brenda interrupted. 'This is a newish spirit and she – I think it's a she --, is not at rest. She wants to move on but can't as there's something that needs to be resolved before she can pass over. Have you ever felt or heard an unexplained noise here?' Before Skye had a chance to answer, Anne-Marie said 'What about the scratching?'

'Oh yes, there's that. Now you've really frightened me.' Skye stammered.

Being a very practical person, Anne-Marie didn't really believe in all that mumbo jumbo' as she called it, but felt having a séance would be something to do that would liven things up a bit around here. She decided to suggest it.

'Let's have a séance and see if the spirit would come through. It'll be a laugh.'

'It's nothing to laugh about. There's a soul in torment who is desperately unhappy and needs to move on' Brenda admonished her.

'Sorry love. 'Didn't mean to mock'

Anne-Marie had always enjoyed life but recently her husband Leon, who was only sixty five had decided he was old now and didn't want to gallivant all over the world any more now he had retired. He just wanted to take it easy from now on, having been constantly responsible for his company's value on the stock exchange, he decided he had had enough, pressure in his life, and now wanted to do nothing. This really upset Anne-Marie, who had been, and still was, a lively active person, and was always fun to have around, and she wanted to be 'doing things', as she put it.

'Surely you have only retired from having to go to the office and driving miles every day, now is the time we are free to go on holiday whenever we like. 'We could take one of those long cruises we were never able to before.' she pleaded. But he wouldn't have any of it, and seemed rooted to his chair doing crosswords and reading two or three newspapers a day 'I feel like having an affair' she told Skye, 'but when do I get a chance to meet anyone when I'm stuck here all day.' Skye was shocked.

Now, having something to challenge her, Anne-Marie threw herself into organising the séance and asked other residents from the Ridge along for a fun evening. Skye wouldn't mind she thought, so didn't bother to ask her if she did, just in case she did.

'How can a dinner lady with a name like Brenda be a medium?' Skye giggled.

'I told her she would get more clients if she called herself Madam something exotic. Got any suggestions? Your hippie mates always changed their names didn't they? I bet your Oberon wasn't christened that, and I'm sure your name isn't really Skye is it?' Anne- Marie probed.

'No it's Maureen. But I don't ever want to be called that again. Promise me you won't tell anyone, 'cos it reminds me of my dreary restrictive childhood. I never managed to find out Oberon's real name. Nobody in the commune knew.'

'Right then girl, who shall we ask to the séance?' An excited Anne-Marie wanted to know, not mentioning that she had already issued invitations.

The night of the séance arrived. The kids went to stay with their friends at the other end of the terrace.

'Best not to have them here; you never know what might happen.' Skye said.

Anne-Marie had rustled up seven interested people from the Ridge who were keen to attend, and it all started off as a merry little group pleased to be at a party, even a small one like this. After a lot of chit chat Brenda summoned them to the round table where the Ouija board had been set up for the spirit to spell out his or her message

'We better get started soon. The spirit is getting restless' Brenda said. There were a few suppressed giggles, thinking this was going to be fun, and they gathered round the table.

'We need to form a circle, so I need you all to hold hands, and keep them joined throughout the session' she instructed. When they all stopped fidgeting she began.

'Is there anybody there?' Then again 'Is there anybody there? This time Anne- Marie could no longer repress her laughter, which ruined the concentration of the group who joined in giggling.

'If you are not going to take this seriously, nobody will come through.' Brenda said crossly getting up from her chair as if to leave.

'Sorry Bren. Promise I won't do it again', said a not very contrite Anne-Marie.

Brenda waited for complete silence before she tried again.

'Is there anybody there? Then again the same question. 'Is there anybody there?' Was there a movement from the glass? It was barely perceptible but the guests looked at each other nervously wondering what, if anything was happening, and what had they got themselves into. Brenda asked again, this time in a voice that didn't sound like hers at all. Then there was an almighty crash. Skye's vases and bric-a-brac started to fly around the room, hurling themselves at the walls. The table practically leapt across the room, knocking two of the guests off their chairs, and Brenda's strange voice shouted 'Get him, don't let the bastard get away with it. Get him before he dies'. Then the table stopped moving: the ornaments crashed to the floor, and the room went deadly quiet. Brenda was slumped over the table with her eyes closed barely breathing.

'Don't touch her' Sheila from number two said. 'I think I saw in a television play once that you have to let mediums come out of their trance slowly, otherwise it's dangerous for them.' Skye, who was looking very pale, agreed, so they all just stared at poor Brenda, not knowing what else to do. Slowly, very slowly, she returned to her usual self and looked around asking them what happened. All talking at once they told her.

' The table moved knocking me off my chair' – 'your voice went all funny' – 'Skye's vases are all broken' – 'That was the most frightening thing I've ever experienced' -'She said get the bastard' and so on.

'Did she? Did she give her name? They do sometimes. That's very interesting'.

'I've just remembered something' Anne-Marie stammered. 'When Gillian lived here she had an odd experience once when she thought she heard a voice saying 'Call her Millie'. She was pregnant at the time, although she wasn't aware of it, but when she gave birth to a little girl eight months later, she did call her Millie.' The guests all looked shaken by their experience and dispersed soon after. Anne-Marie took Brenda home as she seemed wiped out by her efforts, leaving Skye to clear up the mess. Unsurprisingly Skye didn't sleep a wink that night.

The next day it was the talk of the Ridge with all manner of speculations being bandied about as to what had happened. Anne-Marie, ever the practical one decided she and Skye would go to the town hall and the library to see what information was available on past occupants of number eight.

'We won't have to go back too far' said Ann-Marie, 'as he is obviously still alive 'cos the spirit said 'get him before he dies. God, I'm talking as if I believe this stuff.'

They were told either the Land Registry or the Electoral Roll was their best source of information. Land Registry revealed all the cottages had at one time belonged to Millicent Howard and on her death they were inherited by George Williamson, her nephew. He later sold them on to a local developer, Martin Lowe.

'I think we are on to something,' a triumphal Anne-Marie shouted. Millicent – Millie, she's the spirit. I bought number seven in 1950 from, Martin Lowe. He had purchased all the cottages in the Ridge and restored them. His son runs the building business now. Let's go and see him.'

She whisked Skye off before she had a chance to comment one way or the other.

'Hi, are you Martin? – No of course you're not. You're far too young. You must be his son. Is he around?' Anne –Marie demanded.

'Yes, who shall I say wants to speak to him?' a mystified Justin asked.

'A couple from Daffodil Ridge' she answered. He looked worried as he introduced them to his Dad. What was wrong with the cottages he wondered? His father was not averse to cutting corners in his day, and Justin thought he had finally finished repairing his faulty workmanship, but maybe he hadn't.

Martin told them. 'My son has the energy and ideas of a young man so I was happy to turn the business over to him.'

'Do you remember George Williamson?' Skye enquired. Justin gave a sigh of relief and excused himself. As this woman's cottage roof hadn't fallen in so he was no longer interested in what she had to say, and moved off to allow them to talk to his father.

'Oh yes. I bought the cottages from him' Martin said. 'I did them up, put in decent bathrooms and both of us did quite nicely out of the deal. I remember you Mrs Mason; number seven isn't it he smirked? George was lucky' he told them. 'Because his missing aunt's great age, she was presumed dead after only a couple of years and he was able to claim his inheritance early. I believe it's usual to wait about ten years.' Martin informed them.

'That's it. He's the killer. That's the one Millie wants punished' Anne-Marie shrieked. Martin looked worried. Millicent Howard was long dead. She wasn't killed – was she? What rubbish was this woman talking about? Is she mad?' Skye thanked him profusely and dragged her friend away.

'Mum, have you noticed that crack in the wall? It's split the wall paper.' Jon, now thirteen and very much the man of the house observed.

'No - show me?' Skye shuddered thinking I'm sure that has got something to do with the séance. That's where that scratching noise comes from.

'I'll phone the council' she told him. Shaking, she made the call and was told they will be round the next day. The following morning after the kids had gone to school, the council workers turned up.

'That's nasty' the foreman announced, 'that could mean the front of the house is pulling away. I've seen that before in these old places. We'll soon sort that out.'

Skye was in Anne-Marie's house to get away from the dust, but they couldn't avoid the banging and crashing which was getting on their nerves. The foreman knocked on her door.

'I think you better come and see this Mrs McAllister.'

Looking worried the friends held hands nervously to go to see whatever disaster had been uncovered. They saw what looked suspiciously like a body wrapped in sheeting amongst the plaster and concrete on the floor.

'You better call the police Mrs McAllister.' A scared looking foreman instructed her.

---.

Oooh! The excitement the massive police presence in and around Skye's cottage generated. Nothing so exciting had ever happened in the Ridge before, so the residents were hanging about and getting in the way of the police, hoping to see something ghoulish no doubt.

'Mrs McAllister, we are going to move your family out for a couple of days while we are investigating this apparent murder,' and it might be a good idea for you to move at the same time Mrs Mason, as the noise will be intolerable.' a kindly police inspector informed her. 'We can put your families in a comfortable hotel -- at our expense of course.'

'Thank you that will be most acceptable' said Anne-Marie, using her superior 'I would expect no less' voice. Reverting to her normal cheerful way of speaking she jollied Skye along to get packing.

'Leon is not going to be too pleased' she laughed. 'I'd better go and prize him out of his chair, and tell him we are on the move.'

Skye telephoned Jake and Leila's school to ask the head teacher to send the kids home as they had to move into a hotel for a couple of days, when Anne- Marie walked in.

'Wow, you know I should have noticed that long ago? I've been in most of the cottages over the years, and yours is the only one without recesses alongside the chimney breast. I never gave it a thought before. I wonder what else is behind the other wall?' she speculated. They soon found out when the council workers smashed into the plaster: revealing clothing, a travelling case and her passport.

'Clever bloke that Mr Williamson, we are busy tracing him now .He's managed to get away with his crime it for over thirty years, but we always get 'em in the end.' A smug Inspector Johnson informed Skye.

It didn't take them long as George hadn't led a quiet life since he throttled Millie. He was a prominent businessman in the pretty Cornish town he now called home, and was due to be Mayor for the next municipal year. That was not to be. He was marched off in handcuffs in front of his once admiring public, with the photographer from the local paper's camera recording every embarrassing moment of his arrest. Now he was on his way to prison to get his just deserts thirty three years after the event he had almost forgotten and thought he had got away with.

Ha ha! It was Millie herself who shopped you George.

Thinking she may have been traumatised by recent events, Skye was offered alternative accommodation by the council, but refused. She had made so many friends since the séance, and now the spirit was no longer trapped behind the wall, there would be no more scratching, so she was perfectly happy to stay there. The council gave number eight a complete makeover, not just repairing the area around the chimney breast, but redecorating the entire cottage. It looked amazing and she was thrilled as she would never have been able to afford to do it herself.

The event hit the National press and Nick hurried down from York and his new life as a teacher, to check that his other family were OK. He was delighted to see how Skye had blossomed, and how happy his kids were. When he left, promises were made to introduce Jake and Leila to his new family and perhaps have a holiday with them in York.

Skye had been as thrilled to see Nick again, as he was to see her. They may not have been in love, but there was a deep affection between them which was unaffected by their changed lives. To her surprise she found she wasn't jealous of Nick's new wife, only delighted that he had found what it was lacking in his life, and was finally content. She had always thought that she and Nick would somehow get back together again, and it had stopped her starting a new relationship but seeing him again made her realise that she had moved on too and now felt ready to grasp at any opportunity that presented its self, including finding a new partner. There was that nice pottery teacher Robin seemed to be interested in her. Perhaps she should make herself look less scruffy when she attended his next class. She also realised the bond between her and Nick would never be broken. The children would make sure of that, and this filled her with a warm glow, not knowing that on his way back to York, Nick was experiencing exactly the same warm feelings about her.

Clutter

Mrs Tandy was tending her plants in her very small cluttered conservatory that was attached to the back of her equally small cluttered te Victorian house. She was not much of a gardener -- in fact she wasn't a gardener at all, but she loved brightly coloured flowers and bought them when they were in full bloom. Flowers such as geraniums, cyclamens and multi coloured dahlias. But once the blooms had died and she was left with a lot of dried up brown leaves, she lost interest in them. Today she was making a half-hearted attempt at tidying up, as the pile of leaves on the floor had become out of hand and was beginning to look as if autumn had come early to Twickenham. Contemplating whcrc to start, she was vaguely aware of somebody else in the conservatory.

'Put yer 'ands up NOW' ordered a young man in a threatening voice.

'What did you say dear? I'm afraid I'm a bit hard of hearing. How did you get in? She asked apparently oblivious to the gun he was waving about,'Yer left the bleeding door open didn't 'yer? Silly cow.'

'There's no need to be rude young man.' She admonished him.

Oh dear she thought. Now Alice will really have something to lecture me about. She's always telling me not to leave the front door open, but when I'm working in the back of the house I can't hear the doorbell ring, and I don't want to miss a visitor do I? She was quietly contemplating her daughter's reaction to her present predicament, completely forgetting her uninvited visitor.

He was beginning to feel somewhat inadequate as his victim seemed totally indifferent to his threats. She was supposed to be quaking with fear by now and begging him not to kill her, offering him money and her valuables to make him go away. What was he doing wrong he wondered? He had another go at being forceful and in control of the situation. Puffing himself up to make himself look taller and more powerful he yelled. 'Get down on the floor'.

'Oh I can't do that dear, my old bones won't let me do that these days. I'll sit down if you like.' she responded. Judging by his spots he's probably only fifteen or sixteen years old she thought. Joey, one of her five grandchildren, was that age and he was a pussycat once you got past the swagger.

'Why do you feel it necessary to wave that gun at me? It looks like the one my youngest grandchild has. Actually I don't approve of children having guns as toys. It makes them aggressive I think. Did you have one when you were young? She asked him apparently innocently.

Now he was completely nonplussed. OK it was a toy, but it looked pretty authentic he thought – but then he had never actually seen a real gun.

'Why did you come into my house?' She suddenly asked him.

'I was gunna rob yer' he paused, 'I'm still 'gunna rob yer,' he said vehemently.

'Well I'm afraid you're out of luck there as nothing I have is of .any real value.'

An idea suddenly flashed into her mind. 'Oh yes, you can do that dear. It would do me a favour.'

'What?' His jaw dropped. Eh?' She's bloody mad he thought.

'My daughter is constantly nagging me to get rid of all this stuff I've managed to accumulate over the years. I think she's frightened she will have to clear it all when I shed my mortal coil.'

'Whad'yer mean.' he asked, not having the faintest idea what she was talking about.

'When I die dear; do take some of it -- or even all of my stuff, as even I realise it has got a bit out of hand. It will save Alice the bother of having to do it. I don't have any money though, so I am afraid you are out of luck there.'

Now he was completely undermined. He was only just sixteen, and this was his first attempt at his chosen profession -- a life of crime. He was hoping to impress the local gang leader into taking him on after the success of this daring robbery. Not much chance of that now.

'Take some pillow cases from the airing cupboard upstairs to put the stuff in.' she said. "You had better tie me up-- not too tight though – there's some string in the kitchen drawer -- and blindfold me as I don't want to see all my lovely things going into a pillow case and be carted off. What's your name dear?'

'Darren' he replied. Oh shit, that was another mistake. A master criminal would never tell his victim his name as she might tell the police, and as he lived just around the corner from her, they could easily track him down. By now, completely humiliated, he had turned back into a small boy obeying his elders. Meekly, he trotted off upstairs to find the airing cupboard and the pillow cases as she'd instructed. He loaded them with candlesticks, cute little dogs, cats of every shape and size, lots of crystal and dozens of little jugs – Mrs Tandy liked little jugs. He had to make several trips backwards and forward to his house with his hoard which he hid in the shed to be dealt with later.

'Now' she said, 'I will need you to tie me to a chair – not too tightly– then I want you to telephone my daughter Audrey about twenty minutes after you leave my house and get her to come and untie me. That'll give you time to get away. Can you manage that?

'I'll text her.' he said 'No no, don't do that.' Mrs Tandy told him. 'That can be traced easily.' Blimey he thought, she seemed to know more about carrying out a robbery than I do. Who is this old bird he wondered. She's ancient, how does the she know about texting? Maybe she'd been a gangster's 'moll' when she was young he speculated?

'Here's my daughter's number. Call her from a phone box; they won't be able to trace you from there.' As instructed, he phoned Alice when he was well away from Mrs Tandy's house, disguising his voice by putting the sleeve of his sweater over the mouthpiece. Alice couldn't hear him, as his sleeve was too thick so it didn't just disguise his voice, it muffled it complexly. She hung up on him. He tried again, this time trying to put on a German accent.

'Who are you, what's your name.' she barked at him.

'Go to yer Muvvers house,' he told her, 'cos I've robbed her and tied her up.' he said, and hung up very quickly. No wonder the old lady seemed frightened of her, he thought. She sounded a proper dragon.

After Audrey untied her mother, who strangely didn't seem unduly troubled by her experience, Alice called the police. They questioned Mrs Tandy: 'what did he look like? – How old was he? –Did he hit you? – How did he get into the house? Alice answered for her.

'My Mother has a terrible habit of leaving the front door opened. I've told her time and time again not to.' Playing the part of the silly old woman to perfection and inwardly grinning to herself, she answered their questions and told them her intruder was blond, tall and had a northern accent. No --

Darren was mousey, short, and had a strong London accent.

The robbery was reported in the local paper with a photograph of her on the front page proclaiming her to be a heroine, which she denied coyly and when anybody asked her for details about the incident, she just gave them an enigmatic smile and shrugged her shoulders.

After the police left, somewhat surprised at the insignificant value of the items stolen, Alice proceeded to lecture her mother on security and told her she really needed to move into sheltered accommodation. To her amazement her mother agreed. Mrs Tandy had decided herself that perhaps it was time for her to move, but she wasn't going to tell her bossy daughter that. Let her think it was her idea. It was easier that way.

At first she was delighted with the pristine care home Alice had found for her, but the clutter gene is a strong one, and it soon reared its head again. Small creatures started to appear on the mantelpiece and other surfaces, and she felt the wall opposite the window would be improved with a coat of purple paint. She had already arranged for someone to come in to do the job for her, but she didn't tell Alice, and what's more she wasn't going to. It was her home.

As for Darren; six months later he was seen in the North End Road, running a very successful bric-a-brac stall. He had changed his mind about taking up a life of crime as he didn't think he was cut out for it. As none of Mrs Tandy's goods were ever likely to appear on the police stolen lists he felt it was safe to set up his business in the market. After all he did have a large nucleus of stock to start his new venture which hadn't cost him a penny, so why waste it?

The Youngest

Melissa had been in labour for hours and had just given birth to her fifth child.

She was utterly exhausted and acutely depressed, as the baby had turned out to be yet another boy. Her husband had wanted a little girl this time, and she had always wanted one every time she was pregnant, not that she ever told Roy. That was not going to happen now; they would never have a girl, because she had resolved NO MORE BABIES; she was worn out.

Five children was more than enough for anyone, and with all of them being boys, doubly so. With their great thumping feet clomping up and down the stairs or sliding down the banisters along with the yelling: constant talk of football, the TV on all the time with someone either kicking a ball, hitting a ball or putting a ball. There were frequent punch ups that were started in fun, but then turned into serious shows of strength and one-upmanship. How many of her precious ornaments had ended up in pieces after one of these bouts?

Another bone of contention was they were all mirror images of Roy. It was as if had no input to their gene pool whatsoever, and her only contribution was to churn them out, ripping her body to bits in the process. She found herself crying. The nurse, a bouncy jolly girl, said it was just baby blues and it would pass. Pass, how could it with one more potential man about the house? The boys were ten, eight, five, and two, all tall for their age, and now this little one. Would she ever love him? That was a terrible thought. He was a little scrap, totally dependent on her. How could she even think such a thing? Her other boys had all been hefty lumps when they were born; all around nine pounds and all of them had contributed to wrecking her poor body to bits. This one was only just five pounds, but he had still managed to tear her, necessitating masses of stitches.

It was visiting time. She could see her husband Roy with three of the boys peering through the windows in the ward door, -- who was looking after Terry she thought? Her Mum she supposed. She assumed a smile trying to look happy for them. If only she felt it. They all crashed through the door, leapt on her bed and smothered her with kisses. They were hurting her, but how could she be angry with them? The boys loved her, and she loved them with all her heart, but just at that moment she really wanted them to go and leave her in peace.

'What are we going to call him?' piped up Charlie, her eldest. The next minute a huge argument broke out accompanied by the usual raised voices; each one of them had a different name they were promoting.

'Tommy' she said. That surprised her as she hadn't given it a thought until that moment. She had lined up names like Sarah, Rebecca, and Jane, being convinced that finally this baby was going to be the girl they both wanted .A cacophony of sound erupted.

'That's a daft name' 'No, call him Robert, and then he can be called Bob'

'I want him to be called Richard like my best friend'

'He's really horrible, we don't want a brother called that. He might turn out to be like him.'

'Better than your horrible friend Jim, He's really – 'erm -- very horrible.' This from the five year old Harry, whose command of the language was still somewhat limited, as he had always had to shout over the two older boys just to be heard, so the niceties and nuances of the language hadn't had a chance to develop as yet.

So it went on and on, with Roy making as much noise as the kids promoting his choice of name for the new arrival. Frederick was his; it was his middle name and had been his father's and grandfather's name, and he thought it would be nice to continue the tradition. Finally visiting time was over, and her family tumbled out of the door pushing and shoving each other to be first out. I suppose in the wild, it would be normal with males; each one of them vying to be top dog she thought.

'What a wonderful family you have' the ward nurse said.' They are all bursting with energy and good health. You must be a really proud mum.'

Melissa forced a smile and thanked her for her kind words. As the visitors left the ward, it was now time for the babies to start up their chorus, demanding to be fed. More noise. What she would give for some peace and quiet. Tommy decided to be difficult and refused to feed. By this time Melissa was dreading going home and having to look after an exceptionally lively two year old and this new baby that she was not bonding with and probably never would. She burst into tears, and her sobbing and wailing disturbing the entire ward.

Help was at hand. The ward sister decided a bottle was the answer. She didn't hold with this breast feeding lark, as distressed mothers were never any good at it anyway. Never mind nature, that was OK in the past, but this was the twenty-first century, and life was difficult enough without having a battle every feed time and having to worry about did the baby get enough milk. You would know with a bottle. Melissa relaxed when one was produced.

The next morning she didn't feel quite so low, and actually looked at Tommy properly for the first time. He had a really sweet face, and appeared to be smiling. Of course he wasn't, it was only wind. He was far too young to smile. She picked him up and almost dropped him because he was so unexpectedly light after her previous four heavy weights, He seemed to smile again. She held him to her and at last love for this tiny scrap that needed her for his survival overwhelmed her. Holding him tightly guilt swept over her that she had rejected him and promised she would love him forever, the way she loved her other boys and told him she was so sorry she had been so unwelcoming to him, and hoped he would forgive her.

When Roy called in to see her that evening, found the two of them, clamped together, and it brought tears of love and joy to his eyes. So what if it was another boy, they could still try for a girl later on couldn't they?

I don't think so Roy.

The Actress

'I'm expecting a ghost writer called Phoebe Anderson any minute now. My agent thinks as I have just been made a Dame for my services to the theatre and under privileged children through the medium of drama and dance, now is the time to have my biography published in one of those awful coffee table books. He has arranged for this Phoebe person to come and interview me today -- not my idea I can assure you. I'm not looking forward to digging up the past. Me -- a Dame? Blimey!

I think that may be her parking her car – Yes it is. I opened the door.

'You must be Phoebe, I welcomed her. It's lovely to meet you. Do come in.' She's much younger than I thought she would be. Pretty girl: modern looking, you know: black leggings, huge scarf, long blond hair to constantly flick behind her ears.

'Hello Joanna, I've been dying to meet you,' she gushed.

My two large fluffy ginger cats were sitting side by side on my pretty Victorian chair glaring at her the way only cats can, with that 'Who the hell are you' look the species have mastered to perfection. I shooed them off. Phoebe gave me a sideways look then brushed the chair before sitting down. Oh dear, she's wearing black trousers. I forget, not everyone loves cats, particularly hairy ones. I told her today was my birthday and suggested we shared a glass of prosecco before we started. Never mind my birthday; I needed one to steady my nerves.

'That would be lovely, Happy Birthday. You're sixty eight today aren't you? You look a good ten years younger. I'm really looking forward to your story' she said. 'Please go right back to your childhood. I believe you only became a professional actress in your forties. Is that correct?' Without pausing for breath or an answer she gabbled on. 'I'm going to record your words if that's OK with you?' Not giving me a chance to say yeah or nay she switched it on her recorder.

Bit cheeky mentioning my age I thought, but thanked her for the compliment. In preparing for this meeting, I had found recalling some incidents in my past distressing as I had buried them deep within my psyche, preferring not to dwell on the negative effect they had had on me then -- and even now resurrecting them. However, Phoebe seems to be very easy to talk to, so it may not be as grim as I thought it might be. I took a gulp of the prosecco, and launched myself into my history.

'It had always been my dream to become an actress. My mother told me that when I was as young as three, I would round up everyone in the house, make them all sit down, then force them listen to me sing 'Twinkle twinkle little star' and other intellectually challenging songs in a three year olds repertoire. What a brat I must have been? Over the years I went through the usual route for aspiring thespians by starring in school plays, and appearing in local dramatic societies productions. I often received fantastic reviews in the local paper and I thought I was wonderful, and it was only a matter of time before Hollywood called.'

'That's a great start' Phoebe said, grinning from ear to ear.

Her saying that relaxed me, so I gained confidence and carried on.

The first set back in my rise to fame, was my mother. She was not prepared to support me in my dream to attend drama school without taking a secretarial course first. I went into brat mode, shouting and screaming that I would NEVER be a secretary. Mum stood her ground; she had, of course, been subjected to my dramatics over the years and was totally unmoved. She called them Joanna's tantrums. Cheek! My saintly sister Greta never went in for histrionics. She used more subtle means to successfully get her own way. You would think I would follow her example wouldn't you? But no, not me; I always seemed to engage my mouth before my brain.'

'Did you go secretarial school? I did; I bet you loathed it.' Phoebe interjected.

'Yes, I went to a ghastly business school for two years, hating every minute I spent there as it prevented me becoming a star overnight. However, reality checked in soon after I finished the course as I failed my interview for RADA. The rejection was a hard fact to accept, and I had to enroll at an inferior stage school in the suburbs. The school was run by Mary Delmar, a professional actress, or so she said, but I wasn't able to find out anything she had actually appeared in, only a reference to her drama school. Actually she wasn't a bad teacher. What is it they say? 'Those who can, do -- Those who can't teach.' Mind you, we did do a lot of that rolling about the floor stuff that seems to be part of the modern way of teaching the art of the thespian. Bit daft I think. We also did that other nonsensical 'Pretend you are a peach' sort of rubbish as well. However, our Mary did know an awful lot of actors who were appearing in West End shows, who would drop by from time to time. I showed off something rotten when they appeared. It paid off -- or maybe on reflection, it was one of the biggest mistakes of my life.'

'That sounds interesting. Whatever happened to make you think that?' Phoebe asked.

'Well, one of these West End types, Ralph Summers, was getting a group of unknowns together to tour with a new play written by a friend of his, Kier Robinson, and there was a possibility of a London engagement should the play be well received in the provinces. He offered me a job as ASM (Assistant Stage Manager) which is another word for a 'gofer', but I was thrilled and gave up my drama course immediately. Mary tried to dissuade me from taking the job, but headstrong as ever, I reckoned I would learn more with a touring company playing bit parts occasionally, than staying at an inferior drama school. Big mistake. I actually learnt more than I bargained for with the company, and that had nothing to do with acting.

'Ralph wanted to meet me to discuss what he required of me as an ASM, so we arranged to meet in a local pub. I thought then that Ralph was 'posh', so I expected our meeting to take place in one that had been revamped to meet the expectations of the new residents in what had once been a been a scruffy part of London, but was now a highly desirable place to live. No such luck. We met in one that had managed to avoid the style police. The wall paper was stained an orangey colour from the thousands of cigarettes smoked there over the years, and it smelt like a giant ashtray.

My duties as an ASM included making sure the correct props were on stage at the right time. For example, make sure the knife was on the coffee table ready for the murderer to pick it up and kill the leading lady, cue the actors when it was time for them to be in the wings to go on stage, check the costumes, no watches with period pieces etc. and - oh joy! – if I was lucky to step in as an understudy if one of the cast broke a leg or something similar.

I had lost count of the number of gin and tonics we'd consumed by closing time and we were both horribly drunk, and I ended up in his bed in a grubby room somewhere in South West London. Apart from a few amateur fumbles, I really hadn't had any meaningful sexual experience at this point in my life.

This scenario was certainly not part of my long term plan for love and marriage. I had hoped for a grand passion as my early introduction to the Full Monty. Ah well! Life has a way of destroying dreams doesn't it?'

'Yeah, it certainly does.' A shadow passed across Phoebe's face as she made her comment. I was curious. What had happened to her? But carried on with my story

'The following morning, I was trying to wash in a pathetic little sink, with freezing cold water and the absence of either a towel or soap, when Ralph grabbed me by the arm, yelling,. 'Get a move on or we'll be late for rehearsals.'

The next thing I knew we were running for a bus. Silly me, I thought a theatre directors, particularly posh ones, would have a car, but no such luck. The rehearsal room was in a dark, freezing cold uninviting hall in New Cross. When we arrived the actors were gathered round for the first reading, blowing on their hands for warmth and not looking too happy with the situation.

To say the play was incomprehensible was an understatement. A handsome ex soap star, Giles Rushton, was playing the lead character in this enigmatic play, (a polite way of putting it) and his face was a study in confusion.

'What in God's name does the author intend to convey here with this gobbledygook?' He asked. Ralph who was also looking somewhat bemused, as he was having the same problem. He ordered me to make tea for everyone, which I think was to divert attention away from his confusion. As the director, the cast would naturally assume he would have some idea of what the play was about. Things started to go further downhill from then on, until Ralph sent everyone home with instructions 'to read the play slowly in order to understand the underlying nuances of the author's words before tomorrow morning's rehearsal.' Oh yeah!

'Did it improve?' Phoebe chipped in.' 'I ignored her interruption.

'You come with me' Ralph said dragging me into the nearest pub. There was a repeat performance of the previous night at his bedsit in

God knows what post code. I really needed to go home for a bath and collect a toothbrush and clean clothes, but Ralph was so forceful I was frightened to cross him and scared to ask him where we were. That should have given me a clue about my lover, but by now I was obsessed with him

Well the readings went from bad to worse. The girls were in tears and the guys were either stomping around the hall in frustration, or sitting around in despair with their head in their hands.

'Ralph, I think you need to call your mate Keir into rehearsals and explain what I God's name this drivel is all about.' Giles requested. Ralph reluctantly agreed, and the following day Keir joined us.

Keir was one of those existential hippy types, whose head was in the clouds communing with some unknown Indian deity. This was aided and abetted by a constant intake of whackybacky, and he only managed to confuse everyone even more, -- and that included Ralph. Giles decided at that moment that contract or no contract, he was off; back to the popular medical soap opera he had left in order to be recognised as a 'serious actor'. However his character, Dr Sebastian Mulholland, had died -- dramatically of course in a car crash --

after all it was 'a soap' where nobody dies peacefully in bed, but he felt sure they would resurrect his alter ego somehow. Perhaps he thought he could play his twin? Oh yeah? Fat chance I thought.

'I bet that didn't happen.' Phoebe laughed. 'I used to watch that show.'

'Anyway, there was a hasty re-casting, and Bill O'Conner, an actor I had not heard of before -- or since come to that -- took Giles's place. At the end of another frustrating day, Ralph seemed to expect me to trot back to his bedsit like a little puppy dog, but I really did need to go home for a bath and a change of clothes.

'OK' he said, not the slightest bit bothered by my refusal.

'I could come back later if you like' was my pathetic response.

'No, don't bother' he replied. 'See you tomorrow.'

I was broken hearted as he obviously didn't care for me. Sounds pathetic now, but I was a naïve nineteen year old then, just embarking on the grown up's world.

It took me hours to find my way home as I had no idea where the rehearsal hall was in relation to my house, (I had booked a taxi to come here three days ago in order not to be late) and It took me about two hours on an assortment of buses to find my way home. Later I found out was only a thirty minute journey by tube. You would have thought I had just come up to London from the Outer Hebrides, instead of being a Londoner. God, I was gormless back then.

.Phoebe was laughing.' I'm loving this' she said. That was encouraging.

The play was eventually knocked into some sort of shape and off we went on tour, first stop Hull.

Ralph and I continued to be in some undefined sort of relationship and shared digs, but I had no idea if he loved me or if there was any sort of future in our relationship. In retrospect, why would I even think that there might be? I was just some silly little girl who was available. He probably had one on every tour he had ever undertaken.

Well, the play was booed off the stage. I was really worried, as it was not good to be associated with such a flop on my CV with my first foray into the professional theatre. The booing began before the play had finished, and if we had had curtains, they would have been lowered. But curtains are not part of modern theatrical productions, so the actors had to slink off stage looking sheepish.   The audience left the theatre not realising or even caring the play hadn't actually finished.

Next stop Carlisle then Coventry. We fared no better at either venues, except the booing started earlier. By this time 'The Stage' had got wind of this disaster on the road, so they sent a critic to review it. The criticism, Kenneth Tynon style, would have been very funny to read if I had not been a part of the disaster, but it upset the cast and me, who were in deep despair.

'Did you all walk out of the production then? My biographer asked.

'Course we didn't.' That would have been very unprofessional. 'I said huffily.

The next performance was somewhere in Wales, but by this time after the review in the Stage, word had gone on ahead of us as it was reckoned to be the worst show ever to have toured the UK this century. This turned it into a 'must see' cult show and the audience was jeering and making fun of every word. The cast gave up sticking to the script and joined in, turning the production into a camp farce. We were sold out for the rest of the tour.

Needless to say, we did not get West End booking. Kier tried to commit suicide after this humiliation, but his attempt to take his life, was as big a failure as his attempt at being a playwright. He took far too many pills, which made him vomit before they had any numbing effect on his senses, so all he experienced was a stomach pump instead of paradise.

'Phoebe was laughing. I suppose it does sound amusing but she obviously didn't have a clue what the embarrassment of being associated with such a disastrous production at the beginning of my career meant to me. But then, why would she? She's in publishing, not the theatre.

Back in London after the tour, I was confused as to whether Ralph still wanted to live with me now we were no longer working together but I was too nervous to approach him about it. I was only nineteen, and in spite of my outward bluster, quite unsure of myself. The fact I was besotted with him, and frightened to say the wrong thing in case he rubbished me didn't help either.

'Where are you going?' he barked at me, when we arrived at Victoria Coach Station

'I don't know' was my weak pathetic response

'Come on then' he said, picking up my bags, not something he had ever done before. He had never offered help on tour, when I was loaded up with props, costumes and bits of scenery. Maybe he did love me? Then we went in search for somewhere to live. Expectations were not high when looking for bedsits in London, and all these years later, nothing has changed. They are either just about adequate; poor; grim, or downright disgusting and always overpriced. We rented the latter. It was in Earls Court, an area full of Australians, and out of work actors, so at least we were in the right place.

'I lived there when I was very young.' Phoebes piped up.

'I wasn't sure what I was supposed to comment on that remark, so I ignored it and carried on with my story

'I now entered the real world of a 'would be actress, the endless rounds of auditions and rejections. I was told 'you will never get a job if you don't have an agent.' It seemed to me – 'you will never get a job with one,' if his name was

Charlie Jacobs. I used to hound him every day, with very little success. The few auditions he did send me to the part either went to: the daughter of a theatrical family: a relation of the producer, the mistress of the money man, or a girl with enormous mammary glands. What chance did I have?

Meantime Ralph was also searching for work. He had more luck than I did, as he had both acting and directing experience on his CV, but the jobs he was given were not exactly Oscar winners. They were the sort of engagements where he was employed to sort out the mess some other guy had made of a production that was never going to see the light of day anyway, but at least they paid the rent. I was beginning to see another side of Ralph by this time. I was still besotted with him, so I refused to accept he was not the god I thought he was .His arrogance manifested itself in his inability to accept that he wasn't always right. His views on actors performances, his judgment of plays (getting involved with his friend Kier's rubbish play was a case in point) his political views were determined by the Daily Mail, plus, he never listened to a word I said. All of this made me feel inadequate, but as his education was far superior to mine, I always backed down like an idiot. I wasn't outspoken in those days.'

'Finally I managed to talk myself into a job working for a film company, as — you've guessed it – a general dog's body, but it was work. I was to report to Roger Lovat--Smith at Pinewood at stupid o-clock the following morning. I was told to get the tube from Earls Court to Uxbridge, then the bus to Iver Heath. Great, but I still had to find out how to get to Pinewood Studios from the bus stop which was worried me.

'The film was yet another saga about Queen Elizabeth and Essex.

With definitive performances of Elizabeth by Helen Mirren, and Judy Dench, already in the bag, there was no way any actress they cast in the role was going to win any accolades. I can't remember the girl's name -- Maria something Irish I think. Anyway, she was another very popular soap star; but up to playing Elizabeth? No way. If her Essex had been an unselfish actor, she might have had a slight chance of giving a passable performance, but as Richard Butler who was playing him was totally in love with himself, so that was never going to happen He was hired for his good looks and popularity with young girls, not his almost non-existent acting ability.

For a brief while the awful Richard made a few slimy passes at me. He couldn't believe any female could resist his charms, so my resistance was a challenge to him. However, the minute he clapped eyes on my beautiful model sister Greta when she visited me on set, all his efforts were directed to charming her. Sadly, she was flattered and fell for him. I did my level best to talk her out of the relationship, but all that achieved was her thinking I was jealous of her. Yes I was, I had always been, as every romance I had ever had ended as soon as my amour clapped eyes on her. But I certainly had never fancied the egotistical, shallow Richard. She was welcome to him. Anyway, their relationship was a disaster waiting to happen. But, then who was I to give advice about men. Eventually, the producers, seeing what an impending catastrophc the film was turning out to be, pulled out, so -- no finance, -- no film – no job.'

Phoebe chipped in. 'We've all met 'Richards haven't we? I was married to one of those. Not a good start for your career. You must have been devastate.'

'I was curious about her marriage, but she was there to interview me, not the other way around, so I suppressed my curiosity until 'prosecco time' and carried on.

After this debacle, I finally managed to get cast in a decent play. It was Oliver Goldsmith's, 'She Stoops to Conquer', a Jacobean comedy, and I was to play Constance Neville, a substantial part. After a short tour, it was definitely going to open in the West End.. I walked around in a daze for days. Ralph was delighted for me, or said he was, and I couldn't wait to start rehearsals.

At the first reading I managed to throw up. It was put down to nerves. However, when I had to rush to the loo a couple of times during the morning, the director was suspicious.

'How dare you audition for this play knowing you're pregnant' he demanded.

'But I'm not' I pleaded

'Bring me Doctor's certificate by tomorrow to say you are not, otherwise you're out of the play toute suite,' he ordered. He was right, I was pregnant. I couldn't believe my bad luck. I was absolutely devastated. My big chance, taken away from me. I thought I would never get another break like that again and couldn't stop crying. Ralph was none too pleased about the prospect of being a father, but, surprisingly appeared to accept the situation more calmly than I did. A baby in a bedsit? What a horrendous prospect, plus losing the first decent acting job I had been offered, I was distraught.

Ralph, arranged a hasty wedding at Caxton Hall. He didn't actually ask me to marry him, he just assumed I would jump at the chance. As for me? I just drifted along with anything he said as usual, and I found myself spouting my vows in front of the registrar without thinking the situation through. I'm embarrassed to remember what a drip I was then.

Phoebe made sympathetic noises, saying I wasn't, I was just young and naïve.' Yeah that's as maybe, but I think I was pathetic.

Our parents and siblings witnessed the farce. His parents were not quite what I expected. They were obviously quite comfortably off, but certainly not rich, nor were they particularly classy as I had been led to believe. His father was a minor Civil Servant and his mother, a teacher. All perfectly respectable; but not quite as high up the social scale as Ralph had intimated. Also their family name was Samuels not Summers.

'Are your family Jewish?' I asked in all innocence.

'No they are not' he replied vehemently.

'What's wrong with being Jewish?' I asked.

The dreadful expletives that came out of his mouth shocked me, and for the first time I reality dawned on me I didn't know this man at all -- I had married a stranger.

Neither his parents, nor my mother seemed pleased about their forthcoming   grandchild, and there were no offers of help either financial or physical from either family.

As time moved on, our relationship turned sour. Ralph started hitting me, just little slaps to start with, but they soon built up to really vicious wallops. Never on the face though. Pregnant and still besotted with a man who didn't seem interested in me, my world was beginning to look very dark. It didn't matter what I said or did, it seemed to make him angry. I didn't speak to anyone about his behaviour as I felt it was my fault somehow. In retrospect, it was my fault. I should never have put up with such abuse.

Phoebe looked upset. 'People didn't talk about it in then did they?' she remarked. 'My Mum would have said it was my fault for upsetting him' she told me. I had a feeling she knew exactly how I felt from her own experience.

We were both very quiet for a while before I carried on with my story. 'Ralph eventually managed to get a Director's job, which was a great relief, as we were right out of money' However, what he omitted to tell me was the company would be on tour for six months, leaving me on my own, pregnant, stuck in a poky one room flat, with an unreliable hot water system. Very soon his contact with me became very spasmodic, and his financial contributions even more so.

I gave birth prematurely to a little girl I called Petra.

Nothing quite prepares you for the overwhelming love you feel for your baby. Everything in your life from that moment on will be for this child. You as a person are no longer the centre of the universe, as he or she has become that. The need to provide for this small scrap overrides any other emotion or desire you may feel. Ralph hadn't contacted me for weeks, so I had to inform him of the birth of his child by writing to his tour manager asking him to tell him he was a father, but he still didn't bother to call me.

It proved to be impossible to care for a baby in a room with no running hot water so I had to move back to my Mum's, who was not overjoyed at the idea. She grudgingly offered to look after Petra for two days a week, so I could work to pay her for our keep.

'Forget all that actress nonsense' she said 'Get yourself an office job. You are trained for it after all.' I couldn't forgive her for a long time for the delight with which she said that. I cannot begin to tell you how I hated that dreary office and the boring people who worked there and I was becoming seriously depressed.

Ralph did eventually surface when Petra was six months old -- no explanation as to why he hadn't been in touch, and I didn't bother to ask him as I thought he would only come out with a load of lies -- or else abuse me. He seemed to respond to Petra's giggles, but ignored her if she cried, but as to doing anything for her, like feeding her, bathing her, or changing her nappy? – No way.

'That must have been unsettling for you.' My interviewer said.

'Yes, it wasn't the happiest time of my life'. I replied.

The three of us lived in Mum's house for a while, but then she gave us a month's notice to find somewhere else to live. She had never liked Ralph, as apart from his total neglect of his responsibilities, she thought there was something a bit creepy about him. She also wanted to move her latest paramour into the house, which was hers after all. I hadn't told her about the abuse. I was too ashamed.

We managed to find a pokey one bedroom flat miles outside of central London, which made it difficult for Ralph to look for work. No Internet in those days. He started hitting me again, and then by way of an apology, would make love to me, or maybe I should say had sex with me, as love didn't seem to be quite the feeling he conveyed during the act. Had he ever loved me? I don't really think so. Had I really loved him? No of course not. I was besotted with him, that was for sure, but that isn't love. I think I was in awe of him, because being an Oxford graduate he was way ahead of me educationally, but that's not love either. By this time the scales had definitely fallen from my eyes, and any feelings I ever had for him finally dissipated.

I was shocked by the vitriolic bigotry that he expressed about the Jews which he also applied to homosexuals would you believe? For somebody working in the theatre that was ludicrous, as a very large percentage of actors and directors were gay. I started to think Why on earth was still with this prig who didn't support me at all and only made me miserable? The only good that had come out of this whole episode was my darling daughter. I started to think the unthinkable, that I might be better off on my own, and eventually I bravely asked him for a divorce, which he was only too pleased to grant me. I couldn't afford the rent on the flat, so once again it was back to mum's.'

'Soon after my sister also returned to our childhood home, which was not large; the dreadful Richard, having spent all her money dumped her. Now there's a surprise! Poor Mum. She had started to make a life for herself with new friends and interests; there was even a new man on the scene. You can imagine how peeved she felt when both her daughters, one of them with a baby, took over her house.

Greta and I had never been the best of friends, and we kept falling out, mainly over the bathroom. This sent my Mother into orbit, shouting at both of us, the way she used to when we were kids. It was like a house full of Banshees. Her new man took to the hills, as he was a peaceful soul. He had recently come out of a volatile relationship, and had no desire to repeat the experience. Pity, he was really nice. Three dumped women in one small house. Not good! Also not good, was my lousy job working for a distribution company, sending out Invoices. Mind numbing boredom all day, followed by complaints from my Mum when I got home. Petra had done this, hadn't done that etc. Mum really did not want to be looking after a small tyrant. She had already done that with Greta and me and wanted some time for herself now, and who could blame her?

Greta started to talk a bit about her time with the dreadful Richard. She really is very beautiful, which gave him a lot of kudos when they were out attending functions together. They were constantly featured in those celeb magazines, as one of the most glamorous couples in London. But, he didn't have any money, or if he did, he certainly didn't spend it on her. He was doing the rounds of auditions, taking the producers out to lunch, or to his club: spending money as if it was going out of fashion, thinking his networking would give him a chance of getting a starring role.

It didn't and the money wasn't his, it was Greta's.

'When I tackled him about it, he dumped me' she told me. 'Then immediately took up with another model, who carried on where I left off, -- paying for everything.' Poor Greta, what a creep.

'Shall we take a break now' Phoebe asked.

'I have gone on for rather a long time. Apologies. I'll get some coffee on the go. Are you hungry? I asked her.

'No, coffee will be fine.' She said.

We finished off the rest of the prosecco and stretched our legs by walking round my pretty garden. When we returned to the living room, my cats had reclaimed the chair, defying me to challenge them. I shooed them off -- again.

I resumed the interview, telling Phoebe how the years went by almost unnoticed except for Petra's birthdays. She had started school, and looked really cute in her new uniform. I was working flexi time at the awful office so I was able to work longer hours for more money when she was at school, which pleased Mum. After a while one of the lads at work, Stephen, started 'chatting me up'. I told him about Petra, but that didn't seem to deter him, so I decided to go on a date with him as I needed to get back in the game again. That romance – ha ha – didn't last long. I then went out with a series of uninteresting guys, until I met William. That sounds as if love had arrived at last. It hadn't -- it was just he had a bit more going for him than his predecessors. Another couple of years drifted by, and William started to talk about marriage. Before I knew what had happened, I was engaged. I think I had been living in daze the past few years. An overwhelming apathy and boredom had enveloped me, robbing me of any ambition or drive. I just let things happen to me without giving any thought to what I really wanted. I had just hit thirty, so it really was wake up time. I decided if I didn't take charge of my life now, it would be too late.

My ambition was to be an actress, so why was I working in some crummy office? Why was I engaged to William when I didn't love him? Why was I still living in my Mothers' house in a dreary

London suburb? (Back then the outer suburbs of London were unbelievably dull.) I had to jolt myself out of this fog and I found myself sobbing uncontrollably at the loss of my youth. When I finally pulled myself together and dried my eyes, I leapt into action. Next morning I phoned William telling him it was all over: I told Mum I was going up to town to find somewhere to live, and asked her - or rather told her - to look after Petra for a couple of days, not giving her a chance to say no. I telephoned the office and told them what they could do with their dreary job, and off I went to Earls Court and booked into a hotel.

'I feel we have arrived at one of the most important moments of your life is that right?' Phoebe questioned me, sounding quite excited.

'Actually it is the most important, as none of the following years would have happened if I hadn't made that break.' I told her. Feeling invigorated back in a place in London where 'life' happened I went into a café I had frequented in the past. Then I had the most extraordinary bit of luck. I got chatting to a couple of Aussies in the café, who told me they were unexpectedly leaving the UK at the week-end; because of a family crisis, and they asked me if I wanted to rent their flat? You bet I did and it wasn't even expensive. We didn't mention the change of tenant to the landlord. Fortunately I don't think he really cared as long as he got his rent. It was all cash in those days, so there was no name on a cheque to give the game away. A year later he did seem surprised when I finally met him (I had to call him to sort out a leak) and he did ask me how long I had lived there, and had we met before? But thankfully he didn't throw us out.

I found a school, and booked Petra in to start in two weeks' time. I knew she was going to make a huge fuss about leaving her over indulgent Nan, but I didn't care. I signed on at the Job Centre with my new address. Put in a claim for Social Security straight away, as I knew it would take ages before I would be paid. Then round to The College of Further Education, (that's what they were called in those days) and signed up for Drama English A level classes. Whatever had made me think in the past that producers would come running to some stupid woman with nothing on her CV to recommend her, and no knowledge of the English classics? I needed to rectify that ASAP.

I couldn't believe it. I achieved more that day, than in the last five years of my life. I felt alive again and found myself smiling in the street. People smiled back at me sharing my joy. I went into the pub that night, and had a ball. I couldn't remember the last time I had laughed so much. I didn't wait to be spoken to, I started conversations myself, something I would never have done in the past, but that was the old life, this was the new one.

Now came the hard part -- going back to pick up Petra.

As I anticipated, she screamed, she threw things at me, she howled. In fact she behaved exactly the way I had when I was a young. I didn't care; it would be for the best eventually. She hated the flat; she hated the school, she demanded to go back to my mother's to live, but when she realised I wasn't interested in her histrionics, she stopped showing off, and got on with it.

We had an odd assortment of lodgers in the flat to help out with the rent. One of them, Sadie, was great fun, but a bad payer. She had cleared the fridge, and owed me two months' money when she left. The next one, a student called Ruth, was deadly serious, and made me feel frivolous and shallow if I laughed. I was delighted when she moved on. I was half hoping that one of my lodgers might offer to baby sit sometimes, so I could get out once in a while, but that never happened.

Then the heavens smiled on me again; I met Sarah who was a dance teacher. She had replied to my ad for a new flat mate. Petra took to her from day one, which was a great relief, as she could be a right little madam if she didn't like our lodgers. Sarah suggested we teamed up to run a dance and drama class for very young children, a fabulous idea, so we wasted no time and hired a hall that very day. We found a printer to produce flyers, and Sarah's mother lent us the money to get us started. She was an actress called Patricia Rowlands; never in a starring role, but one of those faces you would instantly recognise on TV, but never knew their name.

'It's best not to be a star,' she told me. 'Make yourself reliable, always turn up on time, know our lines, and listen to the director and you will never be out of work.' Wise words: I was now beginning to listen and learn, and not think that I knew everything.

Five years have passed since my escape from the suburbs. I now have two A levels, one in English Literature, the other in Drama. Sarah and I were still running our little drama and dance classes for young kids which I loved and it paid the rent. It was very popular with the mums in the area and we had a waiting list for any vacancies that might occur.

I wanted to teach drama to adults as well as children, but the only way I could do that was with a degree, and I didn't have either the time or the money to achieve that. I doubt if Mary Delmar had a one, but things were different when she started her school. Petra came along to the classes with me, to help, although she was not much more than a child herself. She was determined to go to university to study English and Drama. I was envious' of her, and wished I had been able to have done the same. Too late now: entirely my own fault for shacking up with the wrong man.

Phoebe realised I was on a roll, so didn't interrupt me once.

The next five years were not all roses and I was always short of money, but boy, were they exhilarating. Mum had Petra to stay for the odd week- end, which gave me some time to let my hair down. Mum, bless her, thought I was studying. I had a succession of boyfriends, mostly Australian – except for Martin who wasn't, though he said he was: 'Bit daft in a place like Earls Court, where real Aussies lived. How did he think he would get away with a phony accent? Well he fooled me, but then I am not Australian, but my friend Bruce was, and he put me right. He told me Martin came from Birmingham so I dumped him for lying to me.

I loved the Aussies. They were so free and easy. The Brits were very uptight at that time. 'Not something you could ever accuse them of these days. Bruce and I got pretty serious for a while, but he was going to go back to Oz eventually, and that didn't appeal to me, so I just had fun avoiding serious relationships, and got on with learning to be an actress.

The years passed, as they are wont to do. Petra was growing up fast, and didn't need me so much now, so I joined a local drama group to continue my quest for experience to go on to my CV. She came along with me, and often played the juvenile lead in various productions. There were a couple of ex professional actors in the company. One was an elderly gentleman of the old school, the other a woman in her early fifties, who had had a nervous breakdown at some point in her career. After that she became a secretary as she felt it less stressful than acting. However, she enjoyed being with the amateurs. These two influenced me a lot. Watching them taught me so much about movement, and most important, what to do on stage, when you don't have any lines to say.

A little girl called Saffron joined our class as her parents were concerned that she was so shy and hardly ever spoke. They felt our classes might bring her out of herself. It was hard work, but we succeeded in getting her to say a few words in our little autumn production. I was writing short plays at that time, giving the children a couple of lines each to say, and Sarah choreographed simple dances that they could all join in.

Saffron's parents came to the performance, and were thrilled with her progress. No wonder the poor kid was so quiet. I recognised her mother Frances immediately. She was an actress who specialised in comedy roles, and her father Ben, was equally well known as a Director. The poor child was so swamped by their huge extravert personalities that she had turned into herself.

Ben asked me if there was anything he could do for me to say thank you for his daughter's transformation. I cheekily told him the drama group I attended had been overly ambitious in choosing Uncle Vanya as our next production, and could he give us a few tips. He seemed delighted to do this for me as he was between jobs at the time. The members of the company were a bit resentful at first, -- who does she think she is, sticking her nose in? etc -- but later, realising what a privilege had been granted to them, were soon kissing my feet.

I knew moving into town was important when I made my break from suburbia, because there was every chance of running into people like Ben and Frances because that was where they lived.

'It sounds as if it was all coming together for you. Was that the case?' Phoebe questioned me.

'Yes definitely'. I told her 'I was cast as Yelena Andreovana. A character who has a way of affecting the household with an infectious idleness and lack of interest in any serious work. I had never read Uncle Vanya, nor had I read any Chekov at that point so I buried myself in Russian literature in any spare time I managed to steal out of my hectic days.

Ben, didn't just give us tips, he eventually got carried away with the whole thing, and took over the entire production.

It was a triumph. We even got a review, -- only because Ben had directed it of course, -- in the Courier no less. I received a brilliant critique, which thrilled me so much; I didn't sleep for three nights.

The following day Ralph turned up. He had made no attempt to meet Petra over the years. She was naturally curious about her Dad, but not enough to bother to find him. Personally I had almost forgotten he even existed. He gushed all over his daughter, and was delighted I had kept his name.' I only did that as it had more of a ring about it than Joanna Brown, and of course, it was Petra's surname, making it easier for her at school.

'How beautiful she is' – he gushed. True'.

'How she was always in his thoughts', -- lies

'How he had tried to get in touch with us' -- lies

'He'd always wanted meet up with her, but didn't know where our address.' More lies. He knew where my mother lived, as he'd sponged off her long enough, so he could easily have contacted us through mum. Funny how he could find us now I had a little bit of success. Their meeting was not brilliant as they didn't seem to bond in any way, but promises were made to keep in touch, which will probably never happen? As for me, I couldn't think what I had ever seen in him. He had lost his looks along with his hair.

'I thought you said he was handsome' said Petra. She wasn't convinced when I said he was when I knew him.

That was the beginning of my transition into becoming a bona fide actor. Ben gave me a small part in a play he was directing at the Wimbledon Theatre. This came with an Equity Card so I could now audition for the professional theatre, After a couple of years, of playing small parts, I was cast as the lead in 'Celia', a TV play of the same name by a promising new playwright, Tom Bainbridge. Before the rehearsals I telephoned wonderful Ben and his equally wonderful wife for advice on acting on TV which is very different to stage work -- which they willingly gave mc.

Phoebe jumped up. 'Wow,' she said excitedly, 'I loved that series and I didn't realise that was you playing Celia. You were so funny.'

I smiled animatedly. I was good at that. 'Came in handy sometimes.

The BAFTA awards came around, and although you are told in advance when you have been nominated, I still thought someone had made a mistake. It was for the Best Actress in a TV play category, so when my name was read out, and a short piece from the play was shown at the award ceremony, I thought I would faint or worse still, throw up. Then the actor took his time opening the envelope to name the winner and it was ME. I staggered up to the stage in the ridiculous mile high stilettos I was wearing, and thanked everybody: my daughter, my Mum, the director, Sarah, the whole world, and most of all Ben and Frances. I made a total fool of myself, but I managed not to burst into tears until I got back to my seat. Then the tears flowed. Petra was crying along with my Mum and Sarah, and even Greta was holding back the tears. It would ruin her makeup if she actually shed them. We all slunk out of the hall to have a major sob in the Ladies, and then sidled back in the theatre our faces repaired. Tom won the Best New Play award, which engendered more tears.

Life completely changed for me after that, and instead of chasing parts, I was offered them – really brilliant parts at that. Most of the actresses my age had had so much work done on their faces; they no longer looked old enough to be anyone's mother, so I cornered the market in mums for a while. At last I could refer to myself as an actress. Would I have reached this point in my life earlier if I had completed my course at Mary Delmar's instead of running off with Ralph? I wonder? But now my name is in lights shining brightly above a theatre in Shaftesbury Avenue, and I couldn't be happier,'

'Oh Joanna, that's a wonderful story Phoebe exclaimed .That's a great place to stop. Shall we resume tomorrow with the next twenty years?

'Do we have to? I asked her, feeling drained.

'Yes, my bosses want your biography ready for the Christmas market, so I need to get a move on.' To apologise for my lack of enthusiasm for her hard work I invited her for lunch the next day telling her I would ask Petra along so she could meet her, as she was very important in my story.

'Thank you. I'll bring a bottle,' she offered.

The following morning a sudden thought swept over me, Ralph is still alive, so I doubt if Phoebe could use any of the stuff I told her yesterday. The publishing company – and probably me as well --

could both end up with writs for bringing his name into disrepute if it was published. Oh dear! I'm afraid I chuckled to myself 'cos I'm not that keen on this book idea anyway, and it will be pretty boring without Ralph being in it. I'll tell her over lunch, but I'll let the wine flow freely before I do. Maybe before I tell her, I can find out about her life. We seem to have shared some experiences -- the abusive husbands being one of them.

Not Quite a Traditional Christmas

'Hi Dad, Happy Christmas, come on in.'

Since my Mother died I had taken it upon myself to continue the tradition of the family Christmas. Can't imagine why? They were always awful.

I paused, ---- What in God's name is he wearing?

'What's with the outfit?' I asked him.

He had on a black fedora hat and long black coat and he looked like something left over from the Belle Époque, but his homely face didn't quite go with the arty outfit.

'It's the new me darling. I loved your mother very much, but now she's gone I am no longer subject to her rules and regulations about what is suitable behaviour for a man of my class and years; so I decided to explore other ways to live out my life.' This was said in a firm challenging voice I had never heard him use before.

I was still mourning Mum's loss, but it seems Dad had found some sort of freedom in her passing. He had always been such a quiet unassuming man, I didn't realise he had felt as crushed as I had at Mum's rigid desire for respectability. As we were the most boringly conventional family in the street, it seemed to me she had achieved her ambition, so I could never understand why she felt the need to continue her quest, making the entire family miserable in her wake? I left home when I was sixteen to escape the petty restrictions and apart from the odd phone call home to let them know I was still alive, I didn't visit them for two years.

Now -- twenty six years on I had my own bolshie sixteen year old daughter Freya, to contend with, and a meek and mild son Tristan who I wished would 'man up' a bit. I took Dad's coat and hat, and restrained myself from making a comment about his green velvet smoking jacket and matching cravat. Not so my kids, they burst out laughing.

'Cor blimey Granddad! Are you off to a fancy dress party later?'

A giggling Freya confronted my Dad. Not knowing what to say I gave her a swipe round the legs with the tea towel I had in my hand.

When Mum was alive we always attended church Christmas morning. I can only think this was what she thought respectable people did, as none of us were religious -- but then maybe Dad was? I'd better ask him.

'Dad, do you want to go to church this morning?'

I didn't know if he was a believer. Strange, we always know about our friend's beliefs, but how little we know about our nearest and dearest inner most thoughts. Not a lot I fear.

The idea of church was received by loud groans all round, but I was feeling the need to return to our traditional Christmas, which contained rules that I could follow as this one was turning into a pantomime. Dad piped up again with another of his newly found homilies.

'No thanks. The only God we worship these days is the God of consumerism, and the only commandment is; Thou shall spend money on things you don't need, on presents nobody wants, and for people you don't like, and buying excessive amounts of food we couldn't possibly eat or need when the world is starving. Where's God in all that?'

My mouth dropped open. Greg, my husband looked at me askance. He and my Dad only ever talked about football when they met, not the almighty and his demise in modern society.

'What's brought on this change in you? I asked.

'Is it that woman I saw you with in the pu...'

My fifteen year old son, realising what he had nearly revealed, tried to bluster his way out of it, but, I was his Mother, and he couldn't fool me.

'You were going to say pub weren't you? When did you go in a pub? You're underage' I yelled at him. .'Did you see him in the Crown Dad?'

'No, - no – 'course not.' But I caught sight of his conspiratorial glance at Tristan whose face was bright red.

'Yes, I do have a lady friend. She's called Columbine' he said - rather sheepishly I thought. 'I wanted to introduce you to her but she is spending this Christmas in Devon with her daughter.'

By now Freya was falling about in exaggerated laughter, revelling in her brother and grandfather's embarrassment, and I was getting more and more steamed up and not quite sure who I was most angry with.

'Well you didn't waste much time getting another woman did you? What sort of name is Columbine for God's sake?' I yelled at him.

'She's a free spirit.'

'Free spirit eh? There's no such thing these days. They all morphed into bankers, hedge fund managers and politicians in the late seventies and I bet she wasn't christened Columbine either. She's probably called Pam or Barbara, is she the reason for your new image? 'I demanded.

'Probably; she has opened my eyes to so many of the world's problems and man's inhumanity to man.'

'So you are both going to resolve the ills of society, by wearing daft clothes that cost a fortune eh Dad?'

'No, but we play our part by supporting charitable groups who help the afflicted.'

'Such as?'

'Oxfam: Save the Children, Shelter; Green Pea...'

I cut him off and rudely asked him if he had enough money left to pay his gas bill after all this altruism? Then, out of the mouths of babes etc Freya piped up.

'It's his money Mum. It's up to Granddad what he docs with it.'

She was spot on. Dad had worked hard all his life providing for his family. What right did I have to question anything he did with his cash or whatever woman he befriended? Ashamed of myself, I burst into tears. After we had all hugged each other – apologised for whatever crime we had committed -- me being the most contrite -- peace was restored.

'When are we going to eat Mum, I'm starving?' Tristan asked.

'Sorry love – right now' I said. I opened the oven door to be confronted by a naked bird. The timer hadn't come on. I should have checked it, but hadn't, inefficient cook that I was.

We all stared at the errant turkey in disbelief. Dad broke the silence.

'I didn't want to upset you darling, but I'm a vegetarian now, so I wasn't going to eat the turkey any way. I was going to feed it to Buster under the table.' Hearing his name he wagged his tail in anticipation of what he thought he was about to receive.

'Sorry matey, you're out of luck' I told him. 'We're ALL out of luck.'

After a brief silence, the humour of the situation struck us, and we started to laugh. Jokes about naked turkeys got sillier and more infantile by the minute but that didn't seem to matter, and we continued laughing all throughout the meal. Surprisingly, that was fine too. I always cook lots of different vegetables so there was no shortage of food. The problem of cooking the obligatory roast potatoes was solved, as I found a bag of frozen ones in the freezer and cooked them in the microwave.

The lack of tension around the table, which was always omnipresent when Mum was alive, was fantastic and it was voted the best family Christmas ever. I even relented and asked Dad to bring Columbine round for a drink on Boxing Day. He did, and she was lovely. Good luck to him.

The Letter

1979 Nottingham

'Whose Agatha Mum?'

Your Grandma. Why?'

'There's an odd looking letter for her here.'

'Don't be daft; she's been dead for twenty years' replied Lily as she emerged from the kitchen. 'What's odd about it?'

'It's dated December 1918 and has a French postage stamp.'

They looked at each other in amazement.

'Well, seeing as Aggie isn't around I suppose we should stop staring at it and read it ourselves.' Sally grinned as she opened the envelope and proceeded to read it out loud.

> *Darling Aggie,*
> *I've had some help writing this letter because as you know I'm hopeless at that*

sort of thing, but these my true feelings that are expressed here.

I imagine you all think I am dead after the massacre at the Battle of the Somme, but as you can see, I am not. You can't call it anything else whatever you have read in the papers about 'our brave boys fought valiantly etc. That's Lies all lies. It was a blood bath. The soldiers didn't have a chance to fight, as they were gunned down the minute they put their heads above the edge of the trench. Many of our dearest friends died that way. Well, miraculously I managed to survive because I decided I'd had enough and ran away. Please don't tell anybody you have heard from me, or I will have the Army coming after me to shoot me as a deserter. I'm living in France now under assumed name, and sadly I will, never be able to return to Blighty ever again.

I had to write to you, or though it is dangerous for me to do so, as I wanted you to know just how much I love you as I don't think I ever really told you.

Something else I'm no good at; expressing my feelings.

I had always planned that if I survived the slaughter, we would marry, but sadly that can never be, which breaks my heart. I just wanted you to know, that I will always love you until the day I die, no matter what happens in my future life. Be happy my darling; please marry and have a family of your own, just think of me now and again, as I will always think of you

Goodbye

Yours forever, love Bill.

Sally and her Mother looked at each other in amazement. Where on earth had this letter come from? It certainly wasn't with the rest of the post. Why would it be anyway? It was dated 1918. The post was not always brilliant, but it wasn't that bad, they were both thinking.

They didn't have to wait long to find out. Their neighbour George from number seventeen called round. They didn't know him very well, as Lily had had a row with his wife Irene some time ago, not that she could remember for the life of her, what it was about, but the families hadn't spoken to each other since.

'Hi Lily. What do you think about the letter?' he asked

'Where did it come from? Lily and Sally asked in unison.

'My Aunt Lizzie died a couple of weeks ago he replied. 'Course Lil, you'd know about that 'cos her brother Albert was your Dad wasn't he.'

'Yes but he's been dead donkey's years, and I haven't had any contact with your side of the family since. Your mum didn't want to know about my kids, her nephews and nieces, and...'

George stopped her in her tracks, not wanting to dig up old quarrels.

'Yeah yeah, that's all ancient history now; forget about it and let's move on.

I was sorting out her bits and pieces, and I found it in an old shoe box where she kept her treasures. There were other letters in the box addressed to her from Bill; it looked as if she had a thing about him which was not reciprocated. But how she got hold of a letter addressed to Aggie, I have no idea'

'Thanks for bringing it round to us. If you can think of any reason why Lizzie had it, do call round again' said Sally.

'Have a 'cuppa with us next time.' Lily added, trying to make amends for the past.

'I'll do that girl.' He said cheerfully'

1916 Nottingham

Aggie rushed down stairs to meet the postman. Surely there would be a letter from Bill. She hadn't heard from him for few weeks, and there had been terrible news from the Western Front, with thousands of soldiers killed on both sides of the conflict. Please God she prayed, don't let him die. Sadly there was no letter, so she began to suspect the worst .There had been rumours that the number of casualties was far far greater than reported in the newspapers. Those reports were all about the brave boys who had given their lives for freedom and their country. However, some of the brothers of her friends, who had returned home, terribly injured, had a different story to tell of bad leadership, and totally unacceptable loss of life. Aggie's friend Lizzie's youngest brother Fred, was killed, as were, most of the other members of the Pals Battalion from Jubilee Terrace, and she began to think there was no hope for Bill. But she kept on writing to him, just in case. That was until Bill's father came to her house to tell her they had heard from his regiment that Bill was missing in action, presumed dead. Part of her died that day.

1979 Nottingham

'I'm off mum'

'Where are you going?'

'To the library, I can concentrate better there. I want to know more than just the basic cause of the so called Great War. How can any war be great? I don't know much about the Pals Battalions either, and I want to find out how they came about.'

'Aren't you supposed to be researching for your doctorate?'

'That can wait mum. My curiosity has been aroused by Bill's letter.'

Sally had always enjoyed detailed research; it was what she did at th BBC to earn her living, and she was excited at having a new project.

In the library she discovered Germany had a plan, devised, by Count Alfred von Schlieffen, to secure their borders against invaders.

The invasion of France was to be preceded by a surprise attack on Belgium which had been declared neutral in 1839, so they were totally unprepared to repel the invasion of the German army which swept through their country unopposed all the way to the French border. The planned attack through Belgium into France would then be completed in just three weeks of fighting, --- or so they thought. This would then be followed by pushing the Russians back from their current borders; thus securing Germany's against future attacks.

On August 4th 1914, Britain, acting in support of Belgium, declared war on Germany -- a war for which the UK was totally unprepared, unlike Germany, who had been preparing for a war in Europe for years in spite of their protestations to the contrary. News had spread of the unspeakable atrocities perpetrated on the Belgium people. The Germans were raping women, and shooting citizens for no reason whatsoever. However, terrible though the atrocities were, the gossip was far worse and wildly exaggerated. Saying they ate babies was one of the 'facts' that people believed. In the light of these rumours, the horrified British public rallied to support the 'plucky little Belgians'.

'Wasn't your Uncle Reg killed in the Great War?' Sally asked her mum's old school friend Lena.

'Yeah, lots of the boys round here were. They all joined the Pals regiment.'

'I'm doing some research on that now. Do you know if a guy called Bill Brown went with them?

'No idea duck. Mum only told me about her brother Reg, but I think most of them were killed in the first few months of the war.'

Returning to the library she discovered the idea behind the Pals Battalions was a clever (or maybe a devious one) by Lord Kitchener to get as many men as possible to volunteer to join the army which would avoid the politically unpopular compulsory conscription. The plan was the men would be far more willing to join up and go to war if they were serving with their friends. There was bound to be one 'gung ho' lad, who would revel in the idea, and his enthusiasm would infect his mates, getting them to join up with him.

Reg, Lena's uncle from number twenty four was the one rallying the boys from Jubilee Terrace. The local paper printed a photograph of him and what he had said to encourage his mates, and called him a hero.

'Come on lads, it's not for long. We're going to fight for King and country, and kill those German bastards. That's the patriotic thing to do isn't it, and we'll be home by Christmas.' However, they didn't tell them which Christmas.

By the end of August, just over thirty thousand men had responded to the call to arms. If only they had known what fate awaited them, perhaps they wouldn't have been so keen to join up Sally thought.

They were not told of the slaughter taking place on all fronts, or about the lack of equipment available, and the superior numbers of the well trained enemy.

There were queues outside the recruiting offices of boys as young as fourteen who lied about their age (they had to be nineteen) in a rush of patriotic enthusiasm willing to join up for what was to be almost certain death. There was another picture in the paper of them marching off to war laughing and joking, and a list of the volunteers that included Bill, but not knowing what he looked like, she was unable to pick him out in the photograph. Poor old Reg she thought. What did he know of the way lads like him were being manipulated by the war lords in Whitehall as expendable cannon fodder.

Did you know him mum?' She asked.

'No love, I was only two years old in 1914.' she said sarcastically.

Sally continued to speculate as to what happened to Bill. Did he survive? Did he stay in France? He wouldn't have spoken French, as none of the kids from his background at that time would have learnt a foreign language. That was reserved for children from the ruling class: moneyed familics and pupils from the Grammar schools who would have been the only ones to have had that privilege. A strange thing happened that day. The Postman delivered the post, and amongst all the travel broachers, Pizza adverts and other junk mail we are all subjected to, was a letter for number thirty Jubilee Terrace.

'Ah! I bet that was what happened to Bill's letter to Aggie?' she told her mum. 'Lizzie was in love with him. Maybe was jealously the reason she didn't pass on this declaration of love from Bill to her friend? Some friend she turned out to be.'

'You're probably right darling, but what's more to the point, I really don't care. Let me get on with preparing lunch there's a good girl.'

Sally was a bit miffed being dismissed by her mother as if she was still a child.

She was in her mid-thirties, a tall blond stylish woman, who had returned to stay with her Mother while she finished a piece of research she needed for her doctorate. There were too many distractions in London and she was not getting the work done was the reason she gave to her mother for coming home for a while. The truth was she wanted to get away from Charles, her so called boyfriend. He was married and after wasting ten years of her life on him she realised he intended to stay that way in spite of his protestations to the contrary. He was a

Civil Servant, and told her it would be detrimental for his advancement in the service if he was divorced. She had finally acknowledged to herself that the affair was going nowhere, and she was determined to find the strength to end it. Unfortunately she was still in love with him, so decided a period away from London apart from him would help her to make the final break easier.

On her way to Sainsbury's, she took the letter for number thirty and posted it in through their letter box, then before returning home she decided to call in at number seventeen in order to find out something more about Lizzie. The door was opened by George's wife. Sally knew there was bad blood between Rene and her mother, but she smiled at her innocently, asking her if she could come in and talk to them about Lizzie? Taken aback, Rene let her in. They told her Lizzie had never married.

'Who'd marry her, the miserable old bat and she was very bitter that Aggie had.'

'Shush, don't say things like that George' Irene rebuked him.

Sally told them her theory as to how Lizzie had got hold of Aggie's letter.

'Just the sort of thing the old cow would do' was George's response.

Irene slapped him with a rolled up newspaper. 'Don't talk about her like that' she said. 'Aggie eventually married Lizzie's brother Albert as you probably know seeing he was your grandfather.' Irene told her.

'I didn't know either of my grandparents.' Sally reminded her. They died when I was a baby, killed in that raid on the factory where they worked in the last war.

'Oh yeah! Sorry I forgot.' an embarrassed Irene replied.

During her research Sally had discovered that Albert like so many of his pier group had failed the army fitness test because he was too short, and his chest was not the required size. This was as a result of the poor diet and poverty affecting so many working class families at the time. They hardly ever had meat, eggs or milk, as their families were unable to afford such 'luxuries'.

'Albert was very upset, and wanted to go with the rest of the gang, but his poor physique actually saved his life.' Irene told her.

Young men like him in poor health were subjected to taunts and accused of being cowards when they walked in the town, making their lives a misery. They were given white feathers by patriotic women as a symbol of their cowardice --, hoping it would shame them into enlisting not realising they had been rejected as they were medically unfit to fight. He avoided going out in the street whenever he could.

1915 – 1917 France

Bill, soaked through to the skin, squatted shivering with a cold so intense, the like of which he had never experienced before. He was up to his waste in filthy water and sewage in the flooded trench, looking out across a sea of mud, with every tree blown to smithereens, and dead and wounded men, both English and German strewn across the field as far as the eye could see. The trench was plagued with rats, which made him feel physically sick. He had always hated them

What crime had he committed to find himself in this situation? Next to him was his mate Fred. They had been to school together, played football for the same team: worked at the same factory together, chased girls together, but they wouldn't be doing anything else together ever again. Now Fred, or what was left of him, was lying alongside him, dead; shot through the head with a German bullet. Whatever had he done to deserve that? He had never met a German, knew nothing about their country, their language, let alone wanted to kill one before he arrived at this horrendous place, so why did one want to kill him? Many years later, Bill discovered that thirty eight thousand men perished on the first day of the Somme offensive. For what? The battle went on from July1st to November 18th.1916, with neither side making any sustainable gains over all of those months.

Bill had completely lost track of time. He had no idea what day it was, let alone what month. He had been stuck in these appalling conditions for eighteen months now; surely his number would be up soon. Most of his friends, who had joined at the same time as he did were either dead or injured now. He was well aware that desertion was punishable by death by a firing squad, but he decided if he was caught at least you would know where the bullet was coming from, and it would kill you outright. The alternative was waiting for the one that would eventually kill him, or leave him with horrendous injuries. He decided a firing squad was preferable, so he made his mind up to chance it and make a run for freedom. There was no one alive near him and the gunfire had stopped for whatever reason, so that night he crawled over the edge of the trench slithering on his stomach through the mud, the mist and the driving rain, hoping the bad light would shield him from prying eyes. He crawled along like this until he was well away from the front line, before standing up. After running through the fields, for what seemed hours, he came across a barn. He decided to rest there for a while before moving on. On to where? He had no idea. There was a cow and two goats in the barn. They eyed him suspiciously for a minute or two, and then carried on chomping away ignoring him completely. He lay down in the hay alongside one of the goats for warmth, and exhausted, he fell asleep instantly.

He was awakened roughly in the morning by a young woman, who would have been pretty in different circumstances without the fear and worry lines etched on her face. She was shouting at him in French.

'Qui etes vous? Qu'est ce que vous faits ici?

He looked at her blankly, not understanding a word she said. She stared at him.

'Et vous Anglais?' she snapped.

'Yes I'm sorry' he said as he struggled to his feet. I'll go now.'

Then to his amazement she spoke to him in perfect English.

'Go into the house quickly' she said. 'Hide in the loft. I will be in later when I have milked the cow. That is what I usually do at this time in the morning, so I need to stick to my routine so as not to attract attention.'

When she returned she prepared a bath for him: burned his uniform, gave him some of her brother's clothes, made him something to eat, and then told him he had to leave in the morning. Bill was so overwhelmed with his situation he hardly said a word to her other than Thank You.

1981 Nottingham

Sally had completed her dissertation for her doctorate, and was now at a loose end. She didn't feel ready to return to London just yet but couldn't think what to do, next. Maybe a short holiday she thought. Still fascinated by Bill and Aggie's story, an idea started to germinate in her mind of trying to trace Bill or his descendants, -- if he had survived the war that is. It was probably a fool's errand, but it would be interesting to visit the war graves and the surrounding area anyway.

Now she had the bit between her teeth, she decided she would call on every house in Jubilee Terrace to see if any of the PALS might still be alive, or if they had told their families about their experiences, also if they had ever mentioned Bill.

'You can't do that' her outraged Mother cried. 'You can't go calling on people you don't know, asking them personal questions like that. I think you have become obsessed with this Bill character. It's not healthy.'

Thinking she had a point about calling on neighbours unannounced, Sally decided she would put a note through their letter boxes asking anyone to contact her who had any information that could help her with a book she was writing, about the PALS Battalions. That sounded a plausible reason for her request to give her personal details of their family, backed up by the fact she was a History graduate; her mother had made sure everyone in the neighbourhood knew that.

She was pleasantly surprised by the amount of people who responded, and set about calling on them. George contacted her again, and gave her Lizzie's box of souvenirs, which contained Bill's letters to her. Others lent her photographs that she had copied. One was of the PALS, all laughing and joking, dressed in their new ill-fitting uniforms, just before they left Jubilee Terrace for training. Bill was amongst them, and he was pointed out to her. Now she finally knew what he looked like. None of them looked that healthy, she thought. Not really fit enough to go to war. Lambs to the slaughter sprang to mind. She met up with the Smith family, whose son Fred was Bill's best friend. They supplied her with photographs of the boys horsing about the way young lads do, just before they left Jubilee Terrace. God, they were only babies she thought. They hadn't really grown up when they left to be killed or wounded.

One family had kept a blood stained map that had belonged to their grandfather Cyril who had been an officer. The only reason for this elevated position was because he had attended the Grammar school. He told the selection panel he wasn't qualified to be an officer as he couldn't recall there being anything in the school curriculum about how to lead men or kill people. That didn't go down too well with his 'gung ho' interviewers, but they still promoted him.

His surviving daughter Violet told Sally, he was a very gentle soul so all the other lads in the street used to tease him, by stealing his cap and throwing it in the river, and tossing his homework all over the playground etc. This poor soul was going to have to lead men into battle, the same men who had always belittled him. Very early in the conflict, he was badly injured, so was sent home. He spent a year in agony from his wounds, before dying.

The map was a great help to Sally, as he had pin pointed the spot where he was injured. That could be near where Bill was when he made his getaway, so that was where she would start her quest, when she arrived in France.

1916 France

Jeanne returned from the fields, she called Bill down from the loft for supper Her intention was to give him some food and send him on his way as it was too dangerous for her to keep him at the farm; but when she looked at him, he seemed so, pale, thin and exhausted; she didn't have the heart to tell him to go immediately.

He told her how he and his friends had been recruited - totally ignorant of what they had signed up for. Bill told her of the horrors he had experienced in the trenches, the filth, the rats and the bodies of his dead friends all around him.

She told him she had been a teacher in Paris before the war, but had had to return to the farm after her brother was killed at the battle of Verdun. She had spent a year in London as part of her studies to be a teacher, which was why she could speak English so well, though she did have a few problems with his Nottinghamshire accent

'My mother went into a deep depression after Simon's death' she told him, 'and she simply couldn't cope on her own, so I had to come home to look after her and the farm. Then when the battles started with the constant boom boom boom sound of gunfire, and soldiers continually marching in front of their house and stealing their food, the poor woman was so frightened, that the stress eventually caused her to have a fatal heart attack.

'After her death I decided I would return to Paris, but, by now I was teaching at the local school, and I felt I would let everyone down if I left as they were unlikely to find a replacement until the war was over.' However' she continued, 'the school had closed once the fighting started, as the mothers', understandably, were too frightened to let their children out of their sight in case something dreadful happened to them, and I couldn't return to Paris as it was occupied by the Germans by this time, and it would be difficult to obtain papers.'

The following morning before she went to milk the cow, she gave Bill some French primary school books, for him to look at, and maybe pick up a few words of the language .He wouldn't get very far without some idea of what people were saying, once he started travelling to Switzerland, or wherever he intended to go eventually she told him. Back in the loft, Bill was looking at these kiddies books, unable to understand a word. The ABC was better, as at least there were pictures to guide him. The realisation struck him just how ignorant he was, through no fault of his own. He had left school at twelve, and started work in the local factory, sweeping the floor to start with, then later making small metal parts for cars. What else was there for him and his contemporaries to do? Not a lot that was for sure. They were only educated to a certain level, the girls to go into service or retail; the boys to work in factories and on the land. He had never given France a single thought until now. He knew nothing of the reason the war was raging over their country: nothing about their culture; nothing about their language. The only thing he did know it was across the English Chanel, as they had arrived here by boat, -- how far it was from England? He had no idea. He had plenty of time to think up in the loft. There wasn't much else to do there. There was a small gap in the roof that he could look out from to see across the fields. He watched as fresh troops marched to the front to be slaughtered and cars with the Generals travelling in them to have a brief look at the situation, before returning to their comfortable billets away from the battle. Once a couple of Military Policemen knocked on the front door, but went away when there was no answer. That gave him a fright. It also made him think about the danger he was putting Jeanne in by hiding him here. He decided he would talk to her about leaving.

When she returned that evening, he spoke to her about moving on, but she would have none of it. She had grown used to having him around and was determined to teach him at least the basis of the French language before he left. He was a surprisingly quick learner. This amazed Bill more than Jeanne, as he always thought he was thick and was hopeless at learning. Maybe that's what the teachers wanted them to think; backing up what he has started to realise in the loft. His parents hadn't helped either.

'Don't get above your station.'

'Remember your place.'

'Take your cap off when Mr Reynolds comes by. etc'

Who was Mr Reynolds anyway? He only worked in the bank as a clerk. Bill was getting more and more angry when he thought of the class divisions in his homeland, and the way they had been sent to war as cannon fodder. The Officers must have known that the minute they put their heads above the parapets it would be blown off, so why did they give the orders to do so? He had heard the expression, 'Lions led by Donkeys', which appeared to be true. He wished he could go back to England, so he could fight these bastards, but it was not to be.

Jeanne had worked out a plan to allow him to remain on the farm. She thought when his French had reached a certain level she could perhaps pass him off as her French Canadian cousin as they spoke French with an accent. He could then help her on the farm. She then found out the Canadians had supported the English, from the beginning of the war, and were fighting alongside the Brits, so that idea was dropped. One thing she was sure of, she didn't want him to leave. Was she falling in love with him? Surely not? Sweet though he was, he was completely uneducated and she didn't think that was a good idea for them to engage in a relationship which could prove to be a problem later on. He had told her about his love for Aggie, but that didn't bother her much, as there was no way he could return to England being a deserter. Then she thought, what's the point of worrying about the length of a relationship with a war on? We could be dead tomorrow. Seize the moment, and to hell with the consequences she decided. To Bill's surprise she suddenly kissed him passionately on the lips.

Jeanne touched him where no one had ever touched him before and his whole body responded. He couldn't believe the wonder of what had happened to him. He felt he had been transported to heaven His whole body had come alive, and joy had returned to him from the living death he had endured for so long. He actually felt young again. Why did the English always seem to infer sex was dirty? Even Aggie seemed to recoil if 'he went too far'. Too far in her estimation was doing anything other than a chaste kiss. He was in love. Sorry Aggie he thought, but then he was never going to see her again anyway. Jeanne had been engaged to Henri when she lived in Paris. They had been lovers, but he had been killed, near the Belgium border in the early days of the war. The French, even in those far off days, were not as prudish as the English, so being experienced in such matters; she would not have been considered a fallen woman in her country. After all, she was in love with her fiancé, so expressing their love was considered perfectly natural. Bill had a bit of a problem with this attitude to start with, but that soon left him.

1981 En Route

Sally set sail for France in May. She decided to go by boat rather than fly, as she wanted to get the feel of crossing the channel the way the troops had. Seeing as the comforts on the ferry were fairly luxurious, which the troop ships certainly weren't, this proved to be rather a pointless exercise. She duly arrived in Calais, hired a car, and set off for the Departement due Somme. She stopped at the Bray sur Somme British cemetery. No picture can ever prepare you for actually seeing the never ending rows of headstones of the thousands of young men: British, French and German, whose lives were taken before they had even lived them, and she felt a stomach turning mixture of anger and sorrow at such a wicked waste of a whole generation of young lives. She recognised some of the names on the tombstones, and photographed them for their relatives in Jubilee Terrace. There are two hundred and seventy nine British soldiers buried in this particular cemetery, with one hundred and seventy two of them unidentified.

Sally was beginning to think perhaps her mother was right, and she had taken on a fool's errand with this journey with so little to go on. Bill had said in his letter to Aggie that he was living under another name. She kept driving round and round, stopping a various cafés in an assortment of villages, showing them the picture of Bill with Fred. The photograph was old and a very poor quality plus the boys were so young then it was possible they wouldn't even recognise themselves now.

She was heading for a town in Picardy called Corbie to stay the night. She was beginning to think perhaps she should give up this foolish quest and go home – or even a better idea head south for some sunshine, when she spotted an attractive looking bistro and remembering she hadn't eaten for hours decided to go in. A friendly young girl was running the place.

'Hi, do come in. I'm Rosie.' she greeted her.'

There were other English people in the restaurant, and Rosie was switching from French to English with alacrity. One of the English couples, bored with talking to each other, turned to Sally asking her why she was touring this part of France, telling her they were visiting War Graves in the area. Feeling rather foolish, she told them she searching for a man called Bill: whose surname she didn't know, who wasn't a relative, and could well be dead. They made 'how interesting' sounds, then, deciding she was mad, turned to each other for conversation again. Another English couple there found it a romantic story. Rosie, joined in and told Sally she thought her great grandfather was English, but it was all a bit of a mystery where he came from. This was exciting, or though only a tenuous link. She only thought he was English. Why didn't she know if he was or not? Could he be Bill? Was he? Surely not?

'What was his name?' she asked.

'Guillaume le Brun' Rosie said. That was William in English, and Bill's family name was

Brown. Had she found him? Her stomach was churning with excitement.

'This is too much of a coincidence' she said, 'but could you tell me anything about him. Do you know what part of England he came from?'

'No idea' she said, 'we didn't even know he was English for years. My mother is picking me up from work later, I'll ask her.' Sally waited until the bistro closed, to meet Rosie's mother.

1917 France

Bill and Jeanne started to take a chance on him being found, and slept together in her huge double bed. Their original physical need for each other had changed to a deep love. They questioned if it was it the dangerous situation they were in, that had heightened their feelings for each other? They were so unalike. It was not just coming from different countries, there was the age difference, -- Jeanne was a few years older than Bill: then there was the contrast in education, family background, and experience of life. Jeanne had travelled extensively around Europe whereas his sole experience of travel was crossing the channel to go to war, only experiencing the mud and rain in the fields of Picardy. If life had been in any way normal at that time, they would never have met and would have nothing to say to each other if they had. But, it wasn't another time; it was now, with all the horror and danger around them, so they enjoyed each other while they could.

They started to get a bit careless, and went out around the farm together. A group of people from the village passed by acknowledged Jeanne. She waved back, hoping against hope they would not engage her in conversation.

'Who was that man with the school teacher?' She could just imagine the gossip that would engender. They decided they would be more cautious, and concocted a story about Jeanne's brother being home on leave.

Then an even bigger worry emerged. Jeanne realised she was pregnant. She was nearing thirty at the time, so she decided whatever happened, she would keep the baby. Bill nearly had a fit. This war had to end sometime he thought, so what would he be able to do to support a young family in a foreign land, where he didn't even speak the language?

Jeanne was more concerned about how she was going to give birth. There was a midwife in the village, but how would she be able to get hold of her when the time came ad would she keep quiet about the father of the baby. Who was that man living with the school teacher? Could she deal with giving birth without help? Unlikely. However, sometimes nature has its own way of dealing with events. The baby boy slipped into this world, and with very little fuss and just a small amount of help from his father, so there was no need for a midwife. They named their son Gilbert.

Jeanne thought she would have to find a way to integrate Bill into village life, as they couldn't continue to play this cat and mouse game indefinitely. Who knows when this war would end? It could go on for years the way the two armies only seemed to gain a few feet at a time, before they were forced back to where they had started their offensive. She concocted a story of how Bill, was originally from Jersey in the Chanel Islands, an English protectorate and had been stranded in France at the outbreak of war and he didn't have the money to get back home. She said their families had met before the war when they were on holiday and had kept in touch, which was why he had made his way to her family farm when he found himself stranded in France. He had burned his British passport as he could have been arrested as a deserter and shot if he was found by the English Army, or if the German's found him, they would have shot him as a spy. He felt French, not English in spite of his accent, and originally had thought of joining up with the French Army, but they were too far away for him to be able to walk such a long distance, with the fighting going on all over the country.

Jeanne was not too happy about this story, but she couldn't think of a better one, so thinking that the villagers would probably support her because of her decision to stay on as their school teacher, that they just might choose to believe her. They did, -- and hid Bill any time he was in danger of being arrested by the French, Germans or English armies. He became an active participant of any anti German activities undertaken by the villagers, earning the respect of the locals for his bravery and ingenuity – and his French became perfect, -- that's if you didn't mind the local vernacular--, but he definitely didn't sound English anymore.

1981 Corbie France

Rosie's Mother Alice, turned up to collect her daughter, and heard Sally's story.

'Bit of a long shot that my grandfather is your Bill isn't it?' she said, looking somewhat hostile.

'Yes, I am sure you are right. Please don't trouble yourself' said Sally.

'Maman, she has an old photograph of him' Rosie piped up.

'Alright, show it to me.' replied an extremely antagonistic Alice.

Sally unearthed the photographs from her voluminous bag, and showed them to her.

Alice's expression changed to one of mild surprise.

'It could be' No, - rubbish. It's far too much of a coincidence' she said, roughly handing the photograph back to Sally. Nevertheless, she softened and invited Sally back to her house. Seventeen year old Rosie was jumping up and down with excitement.

Home was a few miles from Corbie. It was an old farmhouse, which had been modernised and enlarged, near the village of Bray sur Somme. Sally was trembling with excitement. She couldn't believe that with so little information she had actually found Bill. Alice may have doubted it, but Sally was convinced she had found him. She told Alice about the PALS gravestones she had found in the British Cemetery near the village, with names of many of Bill's friends --- if Alice's grandfather was Bill she added?

Alice started to open up. Sally's French was passable, and Alice's English was on about the same level. Rosie, who was fluent in both, filled in the gaps.

Alice told the story of how her grandmother had shielded an English soldier in the First World War, and eventually married him. She didn't know all of the details about the time during the war, but it was in this farmhouse. She was not impressed with Bill's letter to Aggie, as her grandparents had been very happy together, and very devoted an supportive of each other all of their lives. After Jeanne had died ten years ago, Guillaume, or Bill – that's if he was Bill? - had mourned her loss, until the day he died. He had been a popular Mayor for some years, of the small town that incorporated Bray in its municipal region. He was a Communist, always fighting for the rights of the workers against the ruling classes, and managed to bring in many changes to benefit the people, particularly in education and creating jobs for the village. He never lost his anger against the ruling classes in England, and felt massacre was the only word for what had happened in the Somme. The soldiers' lives were given no value whatsoever by their officers, so his friends, who were amongst the thousands and thousands of young men who were sent 'over the top' to certain death, were expendable. That was the attitude of the upper classes in England. No wonder he became a Communist. Alice loved him dearly, and was very proud of him.

'Did he have an English accent when he spoke French?' Sally asked.

'Not that I can recall,' Alice responded. No he didn't. I don't think anyone ever thought of him as English. That seemed to be lost in the mists of time. Coming from Jersey, as I believed he did at that time, he would have had English nationality. Maybe he could still have been shot for desertion? It was only after my father died that I found Grandpere's naturalisation papers.' she told Sally. 'Grandpere then told me then that was the story

Jeanne had made up, and he wasn't from Jersey at all, but the north of England.' By this time, Alice was as convinced as Sally was that her grandfather and Bill were the same person.

Sally found out that in the Second World War he acted as a translator for the British Army, but kept very quiet about the fact he had been born in the UK. The mistakes he made in English were put down to the fact it was not his mother tongue. Not the real reason of course, which was that he had had such a poor education in his homeland, and having left school when he was twelve, his English was far from perfect, and his vocabulary was limited. He had a Nottingham accent to boot.

'My grandmother taught at the high school and helped Guillaume with his political activity.'

'Did he ever visit the UK?' Sally asked.

'I believe they did, but not until sometime in the fifties. His parents had died by that time, but even if they hadn't, I think if a son they thought was dead turned up all those years later would have finished them off. It was only when my grandfather was old that he told me about his early life in England, and how he met grandmere Jeanne. By this time Alice's hostility had completely disappeared. She and Sally were similar ages, and were rapidly becoming good friends. They visited Jeanne' and Bill's graves together to lay flowers. Sally felt very emotional doing this, and sad that she had only missed meeting Bill by a couple of years. She wondered what his reaction would have been at the idea of Aggies's granddaughter having found her fiancé.

Sally was invited to supper that evening and to stay the night. When Alice's brother Yves turned up unexpectedly he told Sally he was about to be transferred to London for a year, to set up an English branch of his company. He was a stockbroker, and his company had invested a lot of money in the UK, and wanted one of their senior men on site to keep an eye on things. Sally's heart gave a leap, as she found him very attractive, and was very excited at the idea of meeting him on home ground. This was aided and abetted by the large amount of wine she had consumed

'I would be delighted to show you and your wife around the City' she slurred.

'I don't have one of those anymore' he said, 'but I would be delighted if you would be so kind as to escort me around'

He didn't tell her he knew London well, as he was constantly going backwards and forwards across the Channel with his job, as he liked the idea of meeting this girl again.

1918 France

After the war, Jeanne and Bill married. His lack of papers caused a bit of a problem initially, but Jeanne was a very bright lady, and managed to concoct a fairly believable story, to cover how his papers had disappeared. She had been to school with the current Mayor of the town who had always had a soft spot for her, so she asked for his help. She repeated the story that she knew Bill before the war, when her family had visited Jersey in the Channel Islands. She met Guillaume there she said, they had remained friends. The Mayor, deeply suspicious though he was, had heard of Bill's exploits sabotaging the Germans' during the war, so he chose to believe her story. Many people had lost their papers during the war but there were enough Guillaume le Brun's in Jersey to sound authentic if anybody chose to investigate his background. How she got away with this subterfuge she would never know, but it worked. Jeanne had resumed working as a teacher; -- this time at the

High School, and in the early days, Bill looked after their children, Gilbert and Maria.

She was born, soon after their marriage. A man caring for children was very unusual at the time, but then they had never been a conventional couple, and it gave him a chance to study the language more fully.

'One of the first holidays they had after the war was a trip to Jersey. They felt they ought to know first-hand a bit about the place as he was supposed to have come from there.

Bill had become a carpenter, and worked with his friend Jean Claude. They had met when they were making life difficult for the Germans together in the Great War.

Jeanne and he continued to live in the farmhouse, but had long since given up farming, apart from a few chickens for the eggs. Bill made a few changes to the building, but it was Alice and her husband Giles, who completely modernised it.

1981 Bray France

Alice had softened to the point where she invited Sally to stay with the family for a few days. She took her on a tour of the area, pointing out where the principle battles had taken place. They visited the War Graves again, and this time it struck her just how many soldiers were in unmarked graves. Somebody's son: somebody's father, somebody's husband. They gave their lives for their, country for what? To become invisible and nameless as if they had never existed. She resolved to find out who they were – or at least the ones from Jubilee Terrace, and restore their identity. She found herself with tears running down her cheeks.

Alice felt perhaps she should lighten the tour a bit. She had grown up within site of the graves, and really didn't notice them anymore, and the significance of them rather passed her by. .She hadn't realised the effect they would have on Sally.

'Let's go into Corbie, and after we have looked around, we can eat at the bistro.' she said breezily'. Knowing Sally was an historian, she told her the town was quite interesting historically. 'There's a medieval Abbey there' she said.

Sally shook off the sadness she had been feeling, and feigned enthusiasm. However, when Yves turned up, apparently unexpectedly at the Bistro, she really cheered up. She didn't know this was a put up job, organised by Rosie. Being seventeen, she was an incurable romantic, and had picked up the vibes between her Uncle and Sally.

Where was Rosie's father Sally wondered but didn't like to ask? However, Rosie told her without any prompting, that he had gone off with a girl half his age some time ago. Not that she seemed to be too bothered about his absence. She was also curious about Yves missing wife, but decided ask him about her when he came to London. The night before she left, for the UK, the le Brun's organised a big family party so she could meet the rest of Bill's French relatives. Alice's father Gilbert, Jeanne and Bill's first child, Rosie's mother and her kid brother Marc, a couple of Auntie's and assorted other cousins both first and second ones. Poor Sally lost count of them all, no way could she remember their names, but she really enjoyed herself, and appreciated them all coming to meet her. Particularly as her link to the family was so tenuous, --- in fact, there really wasn't a link at all, except her grandmother was once in love with Alice's grandfather.

On her way home, she started to think that Lizzie had done Aggie a favour by keeping Bill's letter. By thinking he was dead; -- after a period of mourning she could then move forward with her life, which she had done by marrying Lizzie's brother, and having children, whereas, if she had known he was alive, she would always wonder if he just might be able to find his way home, or maybe she could meet him in France, and they would marry.

Once back in the UK. Sally headed straight up to Nottingham to take photographs of the village that Bill had originated from, which she sent on to her new friends. She went to the Library, to get copies of the newspaper articles about the PALS -- in fact anything pertaining to life in that part of Nottinghamshire that would be of interest to his family. She then revisited the relatives of the PALS in Jubilee Terrace, giving them copies of the photographs she had taken of the grave stones in Bray cemetery, and found out the names of the men who were missing in action and were without a marked grave. She had decided to delay her doctorate, and do what she had told the residents of Jubilee Terrace, she was doing, and write a book about the PALS Battalions. She wanted to do it by writing biographies of the men, supplied by members of their families, which she hoped would give them back their names, and make them real people again; men and boys who had mothers, fathers sweethearts, not just cannon fodder lying in unidentified graves in France.

Her research took her all over the country. The Liverpool lads had enrolled in their thousands. The PALS 'Hull Commercials Battalion' shared an occupation: Orphans from the Dr Bernardo's Homes signed up together, the 'Glasgow Tramways Battalion' shared an employer, and in the south, the 'East Grinstead Sportsman' formed yet another group -- and so it went on. Thousands of them marched off with their friends with such high hopes and pride as they were defending their King and country by finishing off the wicked Germans and put them in their place. If only they had known what was in store for them and how many Christmases would pass before they would return? Alice and Yves both helped her by photographing other military graves where the PALS battalions had fought, giving her more names to follow up.

London

When she finally returned to London, there was an email from Yves, saying he would be there in two weeks' time. She was over the moon.

She had found out about his ex-wife. Her name was Yvette, and they were childhood sweethearts. They had married far too young, but with both of them being fiercely ambitious, their jobs got in the way of married life. Yvette went to New York to work with a famous fashion house, and stayed there, eventually asking for a divorce so she could marry her American lover. Yves gave it to her willingly, as by now he couldn't imagine why they had got married in the first place, except to please their families.

1983 London & France

Yves was proudly holding his brand new son, who was still without a name. They both wanted to call the tiny scrap after Bill, but whether to call him William, or

Guillaum was the stumbling block. Eventually they settled on the French version, but he would be known as Bill. They had fallen in love the minute Yves arrived in London. They moved in together almost immediately, and married soon after, with Rosie as a self-appointed bridesmaid. They wouldn't have dared refuse her, as Rosie proclaimed to everyone in France and England that she had brought them together. There were two big parties to celebrate, one in London, and one in Corbie.

Rosie was convinced her great grandfather had guided Sally from heaven to the bistro and his French family, and who knows? Maybe she was right.

The decision to have a baby early in their marriage was because Sally was now thirty seven years old, as was Yves. Babies tended to want their Mum's to be younger than that, so they went ahead with the idea of having a child just a few months after their marriage. Sally was also putting her book on the Pal's Battalions together, thinking as she would be at home she would have time to complete it.

Oh silly girl. Did nobody ever tell her that babies take up every waking moment of your life, and turn your brains to mush?

'Jeanne didn't write that letter to Aggie you know Sally.'

'Really! Are you sure?'

'Yes I know her writing well.' Alice said.

'Oh then who did?'

'No idea.' They looked at each other quizzically.

'By the style I would say whoever did write it was English. Who was he? Maybe I should continue researching Bill's life?' Sally speculated.

Overheard in the Cream Bun

I have a small café called The Cream Bun in a dreary part of Croydon which is not that thrilling even in the non-dreary parts, but the rent is cheap and I am delighted to say, gives me an excellent return. My lovely husband Ben is 'in computers' which is great as I know nothing about them, and he has designed programs for me that have made my life so much easier in the café. Ordering on line, an efficient accounting system, and best of all a system for ordering and paying for the sandwiches we make and deliver daily to one of the monstrous glass office blocks that abound in Croydon. I have lots of lovely regulars who come in to eat my cakes; however, there are a few I would prefer not to have. Dave and Tel being two of them.

They are South London wide boys, (that's a polite way of saying thugs) who always look as if they are up to no good, but they love my cakes which is why they come in so often. Dave said they remind him of the ones his Gran used to make. They are one of the reasons (the cakes that is, not

Dave and Tel) why the café is so successful. I make them fresh every day in a kitchen my clever husband converted out of a small storage space at the back of the building. The smell of fresh baking is very inviting, and when it is warm enough, I leave the café door open so it wafts over the pavement. Unfortunately it has to compete with the diesel fumes but it definitely brings the customers in. Sorry, I'm waffling, a fault of mine. Ben's always telling me to get to the point.

Anyway, one day the boys were deep in conversation, when suddenly Dave raised his voice saying 'I'll kill him.'

Well we all say that now and again don't we, but they seemed to be the type who just might carry out such a threat. I am very nosey, and will often go over to a nearby table on the pretext of wiping it down to eavesdrop if I think there is an interesting conversation going on. So, over I went, armed with a, damp cloth and a bud vase with a small posy in it to the nearest table to them, and listened to them muttering about someone who was a grass, who deserved what was coming to him. It sounded sinister and I started to feel nervous. They left soon after thankfully, but I wondered if I ought to tell the police. I discussed it with Ben over dinner, and we came to the conclusion that yes, I should and tell them what I had heard, so, the next morning I called into the police station on my way to the café.

Well, what a farce that was. I spoke to the desk sergeant, telling him I wanted to report a conversation I had overheard.

'Certainly Madam: Your name and address?' I gave him both my home and Cream Bun addresses,

'And the names of these miscreants?'

'Dave and Tel' I replied.

'And their surnames?'

'I'm afraid I don't know' I said feeling rather stupid.

'Do you know where they live?' he asked, suppressing a grin.

'I'm afraid not.'

'You don't know? Um, that's not very helpful is it?' he muttered under his breath. 'Do you know the name of the man whose demise they are planning?'

'No, I am afraid I don't.'

By now, openly smiling, he called another officer over.

'Well constable Jones, this lady thinks that two guys called Dave and Tel, whose surnames she doesn't know, nor does she know where they live, are going to murder (she doesn't know when) , a guy whose name she doesn't know either. Do we have a Dave and Tel on file who would do something like that?'

'No sarge, sorry' he replied, grinning all over his face.

Constable Jones had left the front office now, and I could hear him relating the story to his colleagues, and they were laughing, making no attempt at suppressing their laughter .I fled red faced feeling a total idiot.

However, a few days later, a headline in the local caught my eye

LOCAL MAN FOUND MURDERED.

Thomas O'Malley, a known police informant was found dead, propped up alongside the recycle bins in the Park Crescent cul-de-sac. He had multiple stab wounds, and the surrounding area was covered in blood, causing great distress to the children who discovered him there. There was picture of Sergeant Carl Reece (Yes, the very same sergeant) who was appealing for anyone who had any information that could help the police with their enquiries, to contact Croydon Police Station etc., etc. You know the usual thing the cops say in this situation.

'I'm sure it's the work of Dave and Tel' I said to Ben. 'I bet Carl is wishing he had not been so dismissive of me now.'

Sure enough, right on cue, there he was, Sergeant Carl Russell accompanied by a female officer, in my café, smiling at me in a smarmy ingratiating way.

'Good morning Mrs Prentice, or may I call you Judy?' I glared at him, not answering either yes or no.

'You gave some very interesting information when you called into the station on Wednesday. I wonder if you would be so kind as to accompany us there again, and see if you can identify the two men...'

'You mean Dave and Tel' I interjected. 'Yes,' he replied rather sheepishly.

'Of course, but I must just finish arranging the cakes before I leave.'

Polly, my assistant, was more than capable of doing this, but I took my time in order to keep him waiting. I could almost hear him grinding his teeth. Good.

When I arrived at the station, they showed me hundreds of mug shots on the computer, and needless to say there they were, Terry Murphy and

David Wilson, both of them with a long list of petty crimes to their name. They were eventually charged and found guilty of the murder of Thomas O'Malley, who they said 'had grassed up' one of their mates' as the reason they had killed poor Tom.

'He deserved it. Yer' don't EVER #/grass up yer' mates.' Dave shouted as he was being taken down to the cells.

I was a bit nervous for a few months after the court case, as I was scared some of their mates would smash up the café -- or even me -- seeking vengeance on behalf of Dave and Tel as it was my evidence that had condemned them, but, nothing happened. I came to the conclusion that they either didn't have any friends, or else they were too frightened of getting caught as Sergeant, (call me Carl) Russell who is frequently seen these days, sitting in the window of The Cream Bun enjoying my cakes.

Killer Heels

Oh my God, that was a close shave. I am sitting at the table in my kitchen, back home in Cornwall, my bruised and bleeding feet soaking in a bowl of warm water: feeling exhausted; depressed and humiliated, hoping that I have got away with it, what is IT? You may well ask.

I get very bored here in the countryside, beautiful though it is, and I do yearn for a bit of romance and glamour in exciting places. I was in Truro a couple of weeks ago, and bought myself the most unsuitable pair of red, highest of high stiletto heeled shoes, just to cheer myself up never thinking I would ever have a chance to wear them. Anyway, to relieve the boredom, my friend Sarah advised me to join an Internet Chat website, just for a laugh you understand. That was how I met Winston.

He was everything I had ever dreamed of. He had travelled all over the world: lived in a smart district in London, was a successful businessman, or so he told me, and I fell for him hook line and sinker. He asked me to send him a photograph, but I didn't. I am not much to look at, and I didn't want to put him off. He didn't send me a picture either when I asked him for one. He told me his name was Winston, so I thought maybe he was related to Winston Churchill's family. Yes I know, -- what an idiot, -- but I was in love, and wanted to have some excitement in my life. I didn't know then, that it's one of the most popular names in the Caribbean ethnic group living on London's council estates. Anyway our emails became very romantic, and we longed to meet each other. He said he wanted to marry me.

I am actually married to Brian and we have a couple of kids, but they are growing up now and are hardly ever at home. When they do show up they only want me to feed them, then disappear the minute they've finished eating. I don't think I have had a conversation with either of them since they became teenagers. As for Brian? Well, I think I have become completely invisible to him, so nobody would miss me even if I did leave home.

When Winston suggested we should meet, I jumped at the chance. My friend Sarah, who was as excited as I was about meeting him, suggested Oxford Circus tube station as a good spot as any for the rendezvous.

"That's nice and central." she said. He agreed.

I was so excited: packed my bag, donned my killer shoe, left Brian a note, and off I went. What Sarah didn't tell me is that there are four exits to Oxford Street station, and not having a clue, which one Winston would be at, spent half an hour tearing up and down four sets of steep stairs with my feet in the killer shoes, screaming in protest. I was getting unbelievably hot and was dripping with perspiration with all this exertion, so when we finally met I was not a not a pretty sight.

Winston was a bit of a shock. I recognised him, as he was wearing a red carnation as we had previously arranged.

"You didn't tell me you were black" I said to him.

"You didn't tell me you were fat" he said, and turned round beetling off down Oxford Street at speed. I ran after him but he was a lot faster than me but I eventually found him sitting outside a trendy looking coffee bar. I sat down, -- or rather crashed down next to him on to a tiny little red chair which collapsed the second I sat on it. That didn't endear me to him either, and off he went again .The coffee bar owner yelled.

"That guy hasn't paid for his coffee, so I will add that to your bill along with the cost of the chair".

By this time I realised this was not the romance made in heaven I had hoped for. Perhaps I should return home as the cost of the bill had bankrupted me. You could buy a café in Cornwall for the price I had to pay for that coffee and chair. How can Londoners afford to live there?

HOME!? – Oh my God. I had left a note for Brian telling him I was leaving him for the love of my life. Whatever was I going to do? In a panic, I texted Sarah and asked her to retrieve the letter I had left on the kitchen table telling Brian I had left him. She had a key, so could get into the house. I rushed to Paddington Station as fast as my tortured feet would allow. Why on earth hadn't I brought another pair of comfortable shoes to change into? I was hoping to catch a train back to Cornwall as quickly as I could, hoping Brian wouldn't be at home by the time I arrived and hadn't missed me. Hopefully he wouldn't notice my case and the red shoes when we finally met up. If he saw them even he might question where I had been. He doesn't say much my Brian, and he notices even less, but you can bet your life if he caught site of the alien shoes and a case, even he might actually think something was not quite as it should be.

Well, when I finally arrived at my house, there was Brian with half the Cornish constabulary inside and outside our home.

"Where the hell have you been?" said Brian. "Someone has broken into the house." It was then I noticed the broken window and the open front door. Sarah didn't have a key after all. She had broken the window to get into the kitchen and clambered over the draining board, breaking china and glass in her wake, then exited via the front door leaving it open in her haste to get away. BUT there was no sign of the incriminating letter. Phew, what a relief.

It's all quietcned down now. As nothing appeared to have been taken (now there's a surprise) the police have decided not to pursue the matter – thank God. I am sitting here feeling a total fool. The washing machine is chugging away as I have had to wash all the clothes I took to London with me. Not wanting Brian to notice I was carrying a case, I threw it along with the tell-tale shoes into a neighbour's garden and it flew open the minute it landed spreading my entire wardrobe everywhere. Their dog thought this was a great game and promptly decided to bury some of it, pee on other items, and scatter the rest around the rain sodden garden. Could the day get any worse?

Later on when Brian had disappeared I went to collect my possessions, I suppose I was lucky the house owner didn't notice me crawling round her garden collecting my bits and pieces. I was being followed around by her dog, who thought it was great fun playing tug o' war with my meagre wardrobe, causing some of the clothes to tear. The householder could well have called the police. They don't have a lot to do in the winter, so would probably arrive mob handed again. I really don't know how I would be able to explain that one away to Brian?

My phone is buzzing. It's a text message. It's probably Sarah giving me hell for putting in that compromising position. Oh no. Its Winston saying he might have been a bit hasty rushing off like that, and could we meet again as he still loves me. Nonsense of course, -- especially after all the lies he spun me about being a successful businessman and travelling round the world. He didn't even arrive on the Windrush 'cos he was born in London. It was just another one of his fantasies, but then I suppose he was one of mine.

He was very good looking though.

Maybe he does love me?

Shall I chance another meeting?

What do you think?

Aspirations - Part 1

Dolly, May 1947

I've just been a bridesmaid at my friend Pamela's wedding. She is the last but one – ME being the last – of our gang of seven mates to get married, I'm twenty- three and I am not even going out with anyone. Please God, don't let me stay on the shelf. The humiliation would be too hard to bear.

Pam was match making for me at the reception and introduced me to a cousin of hers. Dragging the reluctant bloke over she said 'This is my friend Dolly, be nice to her.' and then cleared off. I don't know who was more embarrassed him or me.

'Hello' was about all I could manage conversationally at that point.

'I'm Eric. Hello yourself,' was his reply.

He's a bit spotty and ordinary looking and not as tall as I would like, but, beggars can't be choosers can they?

'My name's Dorothy but I'm known as Dolly' I said smiling sweetly at him, but he was already looking across at his mates, obviously wanting to make a quick getaway.

'Where do you work?' I asked trying to keep him interested. I don't know why I'm bothering: he's nothing special to look at, and his name is a bit unfortunate too. Hate that name and with good reason. My friend Doreen's mother bought a pig during the war with the idea of fattening it up for Christmas, and his name is Eric. I say 'is' because it's still alive, as Doreen and her two brothers made such a fuss about it being killed by refusing to eat pork or any other meat ever again if he was. It's enormous and still roaming round their small suburban garden terrorising everyone -- especially me. Anyway Eric – Williams that is, not the pig, finally started to speak. Thank goodness for that.

'I've got a job at Rutherford's. I'm due for promotion soon.'

'Oh, congratulations: they used to produce bombs during the war didn't they?' I said, hoping he would be impressed with my knowledge. 'What do they produce now?'

'Saucepans.'

'Oh!' What else can you say about something as unexciting as making saucepans as a way of earning a living?

Eric, July 1947

'Hello matey' I greeted my friend Terry.

'Coo, I met a stunner the other night. She's got legs...

I cut him off. He's always drivelling on about how many birds fancy him.

Not to be out done, I told him 'I've got a new girlfriend.'

'Ave yer had her yet?

'Yeah course.' That's a lie, but I can't keep 'aving Terry getting one over me can I?

'Pam introduced me to Dolly at her wedding.' I told him.

She's shorter than me, that's good 'cos I'm only five foot six. She's not bad looking 'cept she's a brunet and I prefer blondes. She dresses nicely though, so not 'aving anyone in tow at the time, I decided to make a move on 'er.

'D'yer fancy coming out for a drink one night?' I asked.

'Oo yes please'. She answered quickly -- too quickly I thought. Is she desperate 'cos I'm nothing special? We went to the Dog and Duck told her a lot of lies about my prospects at work. Girls like that sort of thing don't they? Actually my job was hanging on by a thread, as my boss had already given me two final warnings over lateness. So what! I don't care if they do sack me. There are loads of jobs advertised at the Labour Exchange.

We've been out a few times now and I'm not getting anywhere physically with her, so I've decided to pack her up if I don't get any further in the next couple of weeks. I've heard Swedish girls don't make all this fuss about sex Perhaps I'll try and get a job over there. They say travel broadens the mind, but that's not the part of my body I want broadened, so Sweden, here I come.

That night I nearly made it

'Come on darlin' yer know I love yer' I pleaded, but she was 'avin none of it.

'I'm frightened of getting pregnant.' She whimpered.

'Yer know I wouldn't let that 'appen.'

No way do I want a kid, EVER. That seemed to satisfy her -- then progress. I've made it to the Promised Land, the flesh just above her stocking tops. Not too far to go now.

Dolly, October 1947

I ran into Pam in the High Street.

'How you getting on with our Eric then?' she inquired.

'I think he's getting fed up with me.'

'I'm surprised you've put up with him this long' she said. 'Most girls pack him up after a month,' and off she went -- laughing.

Perhaps I ought to give in to him. He does love me and wants to marry me – or so he says – but he doesn't sound convincing. Maybe he thinks if he tells me he loves me, I will let him have his wicked way with me? I'm confused.

A couple of weeks later I gave him a ring as he hadn't contacted me for over a week.

'Mum and Dad are going out tonight, so I can cook you a meal' I told him.

'Going out? Cor blimey that's got to be a first. I'll be round later' he said. I made him a meal of sausage, egg and chips, hoping that would convince him I would make a good wife. The doorbell rang 'Hello darling, come in.' I greeted him. I've cooked a meal for you.' He seemed pleased to see me. Good.

Eric, October 1947

I don't believe it. Her parents are actually going out. I should think they will need a map to show them how to get to the cinema; it's been so long since they've ventured forth. Maybe this will be my opportunity to finally nail Dolly. I know I've said it before but this time I mean it. I'm going to dump her if she doesn't come up with the goods. It's not as if she is riveting company, or even fantastic looking, so unless she gives in tonight then its bye bye Dolly. I rang the bell: her Mother opened the door.

'Good evening Mrs Wood' I said very politely.

'Don't you get up to your filthy tricks while we are out?' she said menacingly.

'Tricks? What tricks? I don't know what you mean Mrs Wood' I said innocently. The old witch hates me.

Eureka, they have finally left the house, Dolly was fussing about with laying the table, so I grabbed her and pulled her over onto the settee and started my seduction plan. I looked lovingly into her eyes and told her I loved her, and I was off and away. She kept saying 'no' but her body was saying 'yes'. Success; made it at last, then, there was the sound of a key in the front door. For God's sake, they have only been gone five minutes?

'What's going on 'ere?' her father's deep voice boomed. Dolly panicked and kicked me off the sofa, leaving me stranded on the floor with my trousers round my ankles, and my somewhat shrivelled manhood on full display to her parents. The humour of the situation suddenly struck me. I couldn't help it – I burst out laughing.

'It's not what you think Mum.' Dolly shrieked. Then her giant of a Dad picked me up by the scuff of my neck and threw me out of the front door.

'Get out you snivelling little bastard' he yelled' and I landed on one of those gruesome gnome things so beloved by Dolly's mother. Bloody painful it was too. Not wishing to be arrested I yanked my trousers up and made a dash for it.

Dolly, October 1947

My Dad's a big man -- he plays Rugby, -- has just thrown Eric out of the front door. I was really worried for him 'cos I heard an almighty crash when he landed, 'You dirty little bitch,' Mum was screaming and calling me other names that I couldn't possibly repeat. How does she know words like that? Perhaps she's not so saintly as she makes out?

'Get up to your room this instance' she screeched. I obeyed, but Mum continued her tirade following me up the stairs slapping my legs with a wet dish cloth, berating me all the way up to my bedroom.

Later in the week I felt I had to get in touch with Eric to apologise for Dad's behaviour, so I asked my boss if I could leave work early as I was not feeling well and went to meet him outside the saucepan factory. I waited and waited outside the factory gates, but he didn't show. Then a Teddy Boy approached me, grinning from ear to ear.

'Are you Dolly,' he asked? 'Your old man gave Eric such a clobbering last night he couldn't come to work today.' I burst into tears. The Teddy boy put his arm around me.

'Don't cry darlin'. I hope you enjoyed yourself before yer folks got home. Come round to my place. I bet I can give you a better time than old Eric can.'

'Filthy pig' I shouted at him, and ran off down the street crying.

Eric, November 1947

I've got another bird now Yvonne. 'Couldn't face Dolly after that last little episode. Talk about a baptism by fire. I've still got a huge bruise on my arse from landing on one of those vile dwarfs her mum has all over the garden. Yvonne has her own place, nothing grand, just a scruffy bedsit just off the Old Kent Road, but it's hers. No parents hanging about ready to burst in at the wrong moment. Dolly keeps trying to get in touch with me, by sending me letters. I haven't answered any of them. No point really. I don't love her.

Dolly, December 1947

Oh God, I'm pregnant and Eric is ignoring all my attempts to contact him. Whatever am I going to do? After I told my Dad, he went round to Eric's house demanding that Eric married me. His parents made a bit of a fuss at first, but then agreed with him that their son should pay for his sins. His dad and mine dragged him out of the pub, and told him his fate, and before either of us knew what had happened, we were marched into the local registry office to be married.

'This is not my idea.' Eric whispered in my ear while we were waiting for the registrar. The service, such as it was, started.

'Do you Eric, take this woman…?

'I aint got much choice 'ave I?' He interrupted.

'Is that a yes or a no?' The registrar asked him sharply.

'Yeah, s'pose.' He replied in a grumpy voice.

When she asked me 'Do you take him' etc, I could barely speak I was so unhappy. This was hardly the big white wedding I had always dreamt of, with a man who adored me and the reception in some posh hotel. After the dreary ceremony my Dad did try to cheer things up a bit.

'Right, let's go to Lyons Corner 'ouse and 'ave a bit of nosh to celebrate our kid's marriage.' he said in a false cheery voice.

'Nothing to celebrate, pair of immoral plonkers.' my Mum snarled.

'Don't you call my son a plonker. If your daughter hadn't been such a tart this farce wouldn't be 'appening.' Eric's Mum piped up.

Both dads grabbed their respective wives to prevent them fighting in the street. That really would have been the final humiliation. Dad herded us on to a number eleven bus and we piled into Lyons in the Strand to celebrate -- if you could call it that. Nobody spoke, not even Eric's sniggering sister who usually has plenty to say for herself. The silence was filled by the sound of seven people munching cheese on toast.

We moved into a couple of pokey rooms in my parents' house. Lots of couple's starts off this way don't they? – It's so we can save up for a flat?

Eric doesn't seem very happy about the situation, but I think he loves me. He hasn't said so, but I think he does. Do I love him? Oh yes. -- At least, I think I do.

Eric, May 1948

Dolly is fussing around with a duster playing the happy housewife in these two small rooms we are cooped up in, and where we are soon to be joined by a baby. This is not the way I visualised how my life was going to be. I thought at least I would have a regular sex life as compensation for being married, but no such luck. Dolly is always worried her Mum will hear us in her bedroom next to ours.

I started a new job on Monday because I was given my marching orders from Rutherford's. I told Dolly the prospects were better which is why I have changed jobs, a lie of course. 'Better not to tell her I was sacked. Davis Electrics is a dead end job, just like the last one -- 'bit like my marriage.

Dolly, July 1948

I have given birth to a beautiful daughter I named Betty. I couldn't ask Eric if he liked the name because he didn't come to see us in hospital once, but I did think he would at least collect us to take us home, but no. I was sitting on the bed with my coat on with all the clobber a baby needs, waiting for my husband to collect me. I felt abandoned. The nurses kept making what they thought were helpful remarks.

'I'm sure he won't be long.'

'Must be held up in traffic love.'

Then I spotted my lovely Dad. What a relief.

'Told you he would be here soon' from one of the nurses. I didn't tell her he was my Dad not my errant husband.

'Sorry 'darlin, couldn't find your useless husband, so I thought I had better come and collect you both and take you 'ome' he said. My so called husband finally showed up at midnight, drunk, waking Betty up along with the rest of the house.

'I was wetting the baby's 'ead' he slurred, but he didn't even bother to look at her. Mum will give me hell because of his behaviour. They hate each other with a passion and it makes my life pretty depressing trying to keep the peace. Whenever Mum's helping me with Betty, Eric goes out and doesn't come back for hours, and is usually drunk when he does appear. She never calls him Eric, and only ever refers to him as 'the filthy beast'. I often wondered how I was ever conceived with her attitude to sex. Must have been a one off.

Dolly, January 1953

The council have finally re-housed us as I'm pregnant again. It's a prefab and I absolutely adore it. Betty is five now and can finally have her own room, so she is over the moon too.

'Isn't it fantastic Eric: don't you just love it?' I enthused to my husband.

'It's alright I suppose. I'm off out.'

I lost it for once actually taking him to task for his indifference to accepting any responsibility for his family.

'For God's sake Eric, can't you even help me by looking after the kids while I sort out this pile of boxes?' I yelled. He looked shocked at my outburst.

'Yeah, you only 'ad to ask.' He responded. Maybe that's where I've gone wrong? I let him get away with murder trying to please him.

After the war there had been a desperate shortage of housing after all the bombing in London, which is why it's taken so long for us to be allocated somewhere to live. Now have our own home I have a chance to treat Eric the way all the Women's magazines tell you how to care for your husband. Hopefully then we can have a proper relationship as a married couple.

Aspirations – Part 2

Eric, December 1960

We've been married now for thirteen miserable years and time has not been kind to Dolly. She's only thirty two, but looks about fifty. I would have left her years ago if it wasn't for my kids Betty and Graham who make my life bearable Because of them I was hoping I would have learned to love her given time, but that hasn't 'appened in spite of all her efforts to please me. You know the sort of thing, making sure my dinner's on the table the minute I come in from work, making an effort to look nice too -- hair brushed, make up on, that sort of thing. I've tried to respond, but sadly it's too late now. I put it down to living with the in laws too long at the beginning of our life together.

Dolly, January 1961

It's my thirty seventh birthday. No sign of Eric naturally. I wish it was my twentieth because suddenly it seems a great time to be a girl. They appear to be as free as birds, not having to grovel round the man in their life as my generation

Skirts kept getting shorter and shorter, clothes more and more colourful, and best of all there is THE PILL. I wouldn't have had to marry Eric 'cos I was pregnant if that had been around when I was young. I shortened the hem of my skirt to try and look a bit more with it. Bit of a disaster really as it was the wrong shape skirt to start with so looked a bit peculiar short. Eric went mad when he saw it.

'What do you think you look like wearing that with those lumpy pins. You need legs up to your armpits to pull that off, and you aint got them girl'.

Pig. I hate him. I wish I could leave him, but how can I with two kids and no money?

Eric, September 1961

My lovely daughter has just bust into the room, grabbed me in a big bear hug, and told me 'Dad you'll never believe it, I am going to be transferred to the Grammar School. Miss Carstairs want to talk to you and Mum about it tomorrow at four thirty.'

'What you talking about, you're at school already. Watch yer wanna go to that posh place for and how much is that going to set me back?' I asked her

'Because I want to go to University and I need A levels to do that. They don't teach up to that level at Waterloo Street. It won't cost you a penny. I'll get a grant.'

I didn't know what to say, so I called Dolly out of the kitchen to come and hear what Betty was wittering on about. She looked frightened when Grammar School was mentioned.

'People like us don't go to University' I told Betty.

'Dad, people like us didn't go to University, but now in this post war world we live in, we do. I have aspirations and I need a degree to achieve my goal'

'Aspirations? What are they when their at home?

'Dad, you wouldn't recognise one if it bit you on the bum' she said laughing and sauntered off. I still had no idea what she was talking about. Dolly and I looked at each other, both looking worried.

'Why do we have to go to see Mrs Carstairs?' she questioned.

'Dunno, but it's at four thirty tomorrow'.

Dolly, September 1961

I was shaking the next day when we went to meet Mrs Carstairs, the Head of the Secondary Modern School Betty attended. She was such a formidable woman and made you feel you should curtsey before you spoke to her.

'You're daughter's a very clever girl you know. Were you aware of that fact?' she boomed. Not giving us a chance to answer yes or no, she carried on.

'I have contacted the local Education Authority who will arrange an interview with Betty, and they will inform you the date when she starts at Gordon Street. Mean time I will give her some private lessons to bring her up to speed on one or two subjects. Good afternoon Mr and Mrs Banks' she barked, and off she went.

We were both struck dumb: then suddenly I felt very angry. How dare she dismiss us like that, as if we were inferior beings? She didn't give us a chance to ask if there was anything we needed to do for our daughter with the change of lifestyle. For example, do we get any financial help with the uniform, as we certainly can't afford buy it? In our day, we didn't have the chances to improve ourselves that are available now. We had lived through a war, which had totally disrupted our education, and afterwards I think we were only being schooled to a basic level to fill all the dreary jobs available to rebuild the country, such as ones in shops, factories and typing pools. We had been turned into the sort of people who would be satisfied with such mundane occupations. Things are different now. There is no way our Betty would put up with being pushed around like that.

I suddenly realised Eric and I were holding hands under the desk. We didn't know Betty was that clever. Maybe Graham was too? What terrible parents we were. We made love that night. First time for months, or was it years? 'Can't remember it's been so long. I think we were clinging together because we were confused and feeling inadequate.

Eric, January 1965

I've got me a dolly bird. Not my old Dolly, but a girl called Samantha with long blond hair like Brigitte Bardot. She's a secretary at the works, and I am in love with her. I'm forty six now, a lot older than Sam. I've never been in love before, and I don't like it as it puts me in an inferior position. I like being in charge where my dalliances are concerned. I've had one or two since my farce of a marriage.

'You better buy yerself some trendy clothes if yer 'wanna go out with me. I aint going to be seen 'wiv you in that old fashion clobber.' Sam ordered me.

I don't want to lose her so I bought a new modern suit from Cecil Gee's that cost me a small fortune, but I thought she was worth it. I have to hide it and change in the car when I am going out with her in case Dolly finds it. Unfortunately it gets a bit screwed up and damp in the boot which spoils the final look somewhat.

Things are not too good between us at the moment, because a girl like Sam requires money, lots of money, and I don't have much of that; in fact I'm in dire straits. Dolly is yelling at me. What the hell does she want?

'Eric The electricity was off when I came home from work. You told me you'd paid the bill, but you 'aven't. What did you do with the money I gave you for it?'

I had to go down to their office to pay it, otherwise we'd still be in the dark.' she said.

Dolly takes my wages off of me 'cos she say's I'm unreliable. She puts money for the rent, electricity etc in little labelled envelopes, then doles out pocket money to me and the kids. Bitch! She has no idea how humiliating that is for me having to ask her for money seeing that I earn't it.

Sam is beginning to get 'narky with me 'cos I don't take her anywhere classy she says. There are lots of Bistros popping up around 'ere, and I think her ambition is to try them all. I'm not keen on them myself. I don't like eating the messed up foreign stuff they serve that I can't pronounce the names of, also the extortionate prices they charge is a disgrace. Give me English every time, not that I tell Sam that.

She's packed me up. 'Says I'm a waste of space, too poor, too common and a lousy lover to boot for a girl like her, and she's met someone else – the boss's son. She has left me with a pile of debts, a broken heart and -- what's she talking about? A lousy lover? She didn't complain at the time did she? The loan shark has had me beaten up. I've got two black eyes and horrific bruises where the sun don't shine, but it hasn't reduced the amount I owe him, so I think I may have to do a runner or a robbery. 'Told Dolly I had an accident at work. Don't think she believed me.

Dolly, May 1965

The doorbell rang and there were two policemen were standing on the doorstep.

'Is Mr Banks, that's Mr Eric Banks at home, Madam?'

'Yes' I said 'Why do you want to see him?'

With that one of them pushed past me and grabbed Eric as he was sidling out of the back door on all fours. Evidently he had been charged with breaking and entering McKenzie's last night, and was supposed to call at the police station this morning to sign a statement. I was dumbfounded. He was marched off in handcuffs.

As he failed to actually steal anything, and as it was his first offence, he has been let off with a caution. Naturally he's been sacked from his job, as who would want a thief working for them, even if he's a failed one. Now he is in the house ALL of the time, sitting there watching football on TV. It wouldn't occur to him to actually run the Hoover over the place or do the shopping whilst I am at work. I'm doing extra hours to bring some money in. I wish he'd leave me, and then perhaps I could get some financial help as a single Mum.

Eric, July 1965

I should never have listened to Dave Richard's. It was his idea to rob McKenzies. 'Piece of cake.' He told me. I presumed he knew what he was doing as he'd been in prison a couple of time for petty theft. Thinking about it, he couldn't have been much cop at it as he ended up inside – twice-- could he? Well it wasn't 'a piece of cake' and muggins 'ere managed to get himself arrested. Dave -- of course! -- managed to scarper. As a result, I've lost my job, and now I've got a record I'm not likely to get another one am I? I suppose there is always the dole. Dolly is giving me hell expecting me to do housework as she is working longer hours to make up for my missing wages. No chance there darlin'; that's woman's work.

Dolly, October 1966

My darling support and helper, Betty, has gone away to university to study something I don't really understand, but I don't like to tell her and show my ignorance. It's something to do with Social Studies, whatever that is. I miss her so much. She's always such fun. There's no laughter left in the house now she's gone.

'It's not forever Mum' Betty said, 'I'll be home before you know it.' but we both know things will never be the same again, and that having got away from this miserable   house, she is not likely to return here to live is she?

Graham shuts himself away in his room, and only comes down for food. He's turning out to be clever as well so it won't be long before he's off to

Uni. Where did they get their brains from? Not me for sure, and definitely not their father.

Actually, maybe I am putting myself down intellectually? I have been promoted a couple of times at work without seeking advancement and I always did well at school. There are a couple of courses available through the company I work for that I might look into. Perhaps I'm not as thick as I have been lead to believe.

Eric, 1967

'Any chance of a cuppa' I called out to Dolly.

'Get it yourself' she replied.

She's getting very bolshie these days: I don't know what's got into her. I think it's our Betty is getting on at her about women's rights or some such rubbish. Betty has changed too since she went to that university. She's not the sweet girl she used to be and she keeps telling me to get off my arse and get a job. That's no way to talk to her father is it, and after all I've done for her? Actually, thinking about things, I ain't rally done that much. Dolly sorted out her uniform for the Grammar by taking a job in the evenings to get the money for it. I was furious 'cos I had to baby sit and couldn't go out myself. Dol then went down to Exeter to help Betty move into her digs. I 'spose I could 'ave done that. Ah well –too late now. I'm off to the pub if I can't 'ave a cuppa.

Dolly, August 1967

Work: home, cook, housework, bed. Work, home, cook, housework bed etc, every day, every month, every year, and Eric always sitting in that chair stuffing his fat face with crisps and bossing me about. It's eating me up and I am frightened of what I might do to him one day, but I don't know how to get off of this treadmill. Did I ever love him? No, I just wanted a husband. Did he ever love me? No, he was forced into marrying me because I was pregnant. He's probably as miserable as I am with the situation, but like me has no idea how to change things.

Betty's home from Uni –as she calls it – and the house is full of joy again.

She said she has an idea that to get me out of my miserable life. When Eric went off to the pub, she sat me down saying she wanted to discuss something with me. I wasn't sure what she was going to say next and I felt nervous for some reason.

'Mum you know I live in a house with six other girls in Exeter, well one of them isn't coming back next term which leaves a room free, and I was wondering if you would move in and look after us? – We would pay you of course.'

'Look after you? I don't understand.' I mumbled.

'We are all useless at housework, hopeless at cooking, and we have endless rows over who should have cleaned the bathroom and whose boyfriend ate all the food in the fridge and endless other drivel. We all really like each other and are sick of this continual bickering which is spoiling our friendship, so we sat down to discuss the future and thought the answer would be to employ a housekeeper. That's where you come in Mum. The girls met you when I first moved down and they all liked you. Would you consider taking us on?'

'Housekeeper? I'm not sure about that' I answered.

'We would all keep our own rooms as tidy as we wanted them to be, but we need the shared areas kept clean and we would like a meal cooked for us at night. We are all eating crap at present and we need proper nutritional food. What we don't want is any interference in our lives and the way we live them. Boys and stuff like that. OK?'

What about your Dad and Graham?' I asked her.

'You leave Dad. He's a waste of space and treats you like dirt and you deserve better, and don't worry about Graham. He's already sorted out accommodation in Newcastle for when he starts Uni, and he intends to stay in the North after he graduates. More opportunities, less competition up there he says, so -- problem solved. 'Graham didn't tell me that's what he wanted to do.' I said to her. I was feeling a bit sad that he hadn't shared his plans with me, but then I had never really felt that close to him, not the way I do with Betty

Mum, you're still a young woman...' I interrupted her. I'll be forty in a couple of months.'

'That's not old today. It might have been in Gran's time, but definitely not now.' she said very firmly. 'You will have plenty of free time to do whatever you want there. Exeter's gorgeous. You could go for long walks in the countryside which is beautiful, and the sea is mesmerising. You could take a course in something or join a group, anything rather than stay here rotting. You could even fit in a part time job if you wanted to'. I said I would consider it.

Why do I need to consider it? I suddenly felt a great weight had been lifted from my shoulders and I could finally see freedom ahead. A new life, in a new city.

What a fantastic opportunity. No more constant demands for food. No more having to live with a drunken slob and living in a constant unhealthy fog from his constant smoking. No more endless football on TV, never mind if there's something on that I want to see. No more insults about my looks and how old I'm looking. It's not as if he has improved with age, in fact I think he is repulsive looking with his hairy nose and bald head. He used to have a fantastic hair, but that's long gone. Why on earth have I put up with him for so long? Why,? Because I lacked the courage to leave, but now Betty has given me the opportunity to do just that and I must grab it. I won't get another chance.

'When do we leave darling? I can't wait.' I called up the stairs.

'I've already started your packing.' Betty laughed.

The Picnic

'What do you want to do today kids?' Debbie asked her children. The summer holidays were half way through, and being the sort of mother who believed in stimulating her youngsters during the school holidays with interesting and exciting experiences. She had only asked them because she was rapidly running out of ideas.

'Let's have a picnic PLEASE 'pleaded seven year old William.

His very grown up and serious nine year old sister, Sybil, put her opinion forcibly in the mix, as she always did.

'Not a good idea' she said. 'You know what a disaster our family picnics always turn into. Don't you remember last summer when you got lost after you ran away from those cows? Then, when Mum had to go to the police station to collect you, they treated her like an unfit mother and probably passed her name on to Social Services.'

'What on earth do you know about Social Services?' her open mouthed mother demanded.

'They took Julie Robinson away from her mum and dad 'cos they said Julie nad Jack were not being looked after properly' she replied knowingly.

Debbie fascinated by this information, started to enquire how Sybil knew this.

William had learned from a very early age that if he kept up the whinging long enough, he would eventually get on his mother's nerves enough that she would give in, just to shut him up. Debbie gave in, as her son knew she would.

'OK, we'll have a picnic' she agreed and decided to quiz her daughter further about the Robinson's when William was out of earshot.

She invited her sister Jane and her three children Stephen, Rosie and Luke to join them, hoping her sister's presence would neuter the constant bickering she had to endure, as Jane's kids seemed to be positive paragons of virtue.

'Oh no, why did you ask them?' from Sybil, 'thcy're awful, and -- and – Rosie's a snob.' She added as an afterthought.

'Luke's a zombie and Stephen's a pig.' from William feeling he ought to add something to Sybil's list of their relation's faults.

'Stop being so rude and nasty about your cousins.' Debbie said. 'Because they're coming with us whether you like it or not.' Peace of a sort restored, she went into the kitchen to prepare the picnic.

'What do you want in your sandwiches?' Debbie regretted giving them a choice the minute she asked. 'Will I never learn she asked herself?'

'I don't like brown bread, its yuk' from William.

'I don't like white bread, it's bad for you, and gives you cancer.'

Where did her daughter get these ideas from she wondered? Did she know the meaning of the word 'snob'? And what was this obsession with Social Services? To add to Debbie's daily agro, Sybil had recently become a vegetarian.

'Do you eat tuna Sibs?' she called out.

'Mum how could you? Of course I don't. It's got a face, and I don't eat anything that has a face'

Grey clouds were gathering instead of the scorcher the weather man had promised. Should she cancel the picnic? Anticipating the whinging that would ensue if she did, she soldiered on making the sandwiches, and added sweaters, umbrellas and waterproofs to the tee shirts and swimming costumes she had already packed, just in case. Jane phoned and suggested postponing the outing to another day but Debbie was having none of it, so off they went in Jane's people carrier. They chose a beauty spot on the Sussex downs, near the sea just in case the promised hot weather appeared. Ground sheets and blankets were spread out on the ground and the goodies were unpacked.

Jane and Debbie stretched out on their sun beds wrapped in blankets and wearing woolly hats as the promised heat had not materialised. They decided not to interfere and to let the kids to sort themselves out as to what they wanted to do. Bad idea! War broke out almost immediately. It was difficult to guess who the instigator of this mayhem was.

'She kicked me', 'No I didn't.'

'He called me an idiot' 'Well you are.'

'He's a liar.' 'No I'm not, you are.'

'I hate you.' 'I hate you too', and so it went on and on.

Eventually, after Debbie and Jane had intervened to break up the quarrel and calm was finally restored, the girls decided to go for a walk, and the boys planned to enact a war between the Zombies and the Darliks, Then, before the 'rules of engagement' had even been arranged, another huge shouting match developed. There were three boys to divide into two equal teams, this impossible so William being the youngest was left out.

'It's not fair. They won't let me play', William wailed.

'Never mind darling; go and pick some flowers for me.' Was life ever fair? Debbie thought. The time to eat arrived around the same time that the sky had turned a threatening black interspersed with a few shafts of sunlight. Jane thought it was about to rain but Debbie felt the sun was going to come out. She was wrong. The skies opened, and pelted them with hailstones, leaving them with no time to get the waterproofs and umbrellas out of the car before they were soaked to the skin.

'Where are the girls?' Jane, said, suddenly panicking.

'Oh shit, where the hell have they got to?

'You swore, Auntie that's a sin'. Stephen, who had recently found God, pronounced piously. Debbie suppressing a desire to swipe him with a wet cloth she had in her hand, suggested he helped to rescue some of the food that was about to disintegrate.

'Everybody in the car' she yelled, and NO ARGUING. They got into the car, but then the racket started up again.

'He's, deliberately dripping water all over me'

'No I'm not'

'He's emptied his trainers all over the floor'

'Tell-tale'

The sisters were both remembering those halcyon peaceful days when they were child free with nostalgia; when a picnic was in the grounds of a beautiful country pub, and copious glasses of wine were consumed in good company.

They drove around looking for the girls, calling their names out of the windows letting rain into the car. The boys got out periodically to check sheds and barns.

'Perhaps they've been kidnapped' said William hopefully.

'Maybe they've been murdered' said Stephen gleefully.

'Oh shut up for goodness sake', pleaded Debbie 'Why are they not answering their phones?

'Surely one of them has a charged battery?' a worried Jane asked.

'I've got Sybil's phone' piped up William. 'I took it for a laugh.'

'Well I'm not laughing, you stupid boy'.

'Rosie has hers with her I'm sure, she never goes anywhere without it' Jane proclaimed with confidence as she dialled her number.

They heard it ringing somewhere in the car.

'I took hers as well because she was being horrible too' whispered William sheepishly, secretly hoping the adults wouldn't hear his confession. They did, and turned to look at him aghast, so he burst into tears hoping this would placate his mother and aunt. It didn't.

Jane and Debbie were beginning to panic. They spotted the Beachy Head Hotel, and decided to ask one or two of their customers if they had spotted three young girls walking on their own. They went in, and there, in the reception area were the miscreants, dripping wet, in floods of tears, milking the attention they were receiving from a crowd of customers surrounding them.

'Mummy, Mummy' shrieked Rosie as she rushed towards Jane as if they had been separated for years. 'We thought you had abandoned us' sob, sob. Oh God thought Debbie, I bet the management have called the police, then, right on cue, two burly coppers arrived and of course, accompanied by a social worker. Sybil's obsession with them meant she had probably sent out telepathic signals to the police to bring one along.

Two hours later they were able to leave the hotel, having finally managed to convince the police and the social worker that they really hadn't abandoned their children: that they didn't take their phones away from them so they couldn't contact their mothers, and yes, it was a silly idea to arrange a picnic when the sky was pitch black, and that the children really did come from happy homes, with two parents apiece unlike the majority of their friends. That didn't go down too well with the social worker, who began a mantra about not judging children just because they came from single parent families. They drove home in complete silence, each one of them vowing, they would NEVER, EVER go on a family picnic again.

Later a calmer Debbie was wondering if she would ever get to hear about the Robinson's.'

In the Shadow of St Paul's

'Do come in Mr Russell; I've been looking forward to meeting you.'

I wasn't looking forward to meeting him but he was a psychiatrist and my GP felt he was probably my best chance of ridding me of the nightmares that have turned me into a gibbering wreck.

'I have spoken to your doctor and I am aware of the incident that you think has triggered your problem,' Dr Jackson said, 'but I would like you to tell me in your own words your version of events from the beginning. Take as long as you like. I don't have any more appointments today.'

I didn't need to be asked twice to tell my story. I had been too embarrassed to relate it to anyone I knew in case they thought I was off my head. Maybe I am, but it was this guy's job to listen which was made a difference. Nervously I began to speak.

'I have an office in an old building that overlooks St Paul's Cathedral.

The word 'office' flatters the tiny room, but it's worth the inconvenience of the lack of space for such a prestigious address, right in the middle of the City of London and it does wonders to boost my business. My company Philip Russell & Son is actually a factory in the Midlands where I manufacture computer parts, but with the ease of modern communications its simplicity itself to keep up the deception that we are a London based company which always carries more clout. The letterhead on my stationery has a soft shadowy grey picture of the cathedral with the office address printed over it and it looks impressive. The 'Son' part of the company name is a misnomer as I only have one son, Paul, and he is not the slightest bit interested in the business that has sustained him most of his life. It paid for his expensive education and financed his time at university. All wasted as he now works as a DJ in some grubby club in Soho. But as 'Son' suggests stability and a business with a future, I continue using it, living in hope that one day it might just might be true.'

'My highly efficient assistant Mandy has run the London office ever since I started the business some fifteen years ago. She is – or was - a rather plain lumpy girl in her mid-thirties, but highly intelligent and forward thinking. She was often ahead of me when changes needed to be made in the running and marketing of our products, which made life very easy for me as was able to leave the day to day running of the business entirely in her hands.

I should have noticed -- but didn't -- how much prettier and slimmer she had looked of late, but I only became aware of the change when she gave in her notice telling me she was getting married and moving to Australia. Being the selfish bastard that I am, I only thought about the inconvenience it was going to cause me, rather than congratulating Mandy on her forthcoming marriage.

'Sorry, am I talking too much?' I asked Dr Jackson.

'No, no, on the contrary. Your background and your life before you were traumatised are all relevant to your present condition. Please go on.'

'Thank you' I replied.' Anyway I was compelled to look for a replacement. Interviews are not my strong point; too wrapped up in myself I suppose to notice qualities in applicants, so Mandy, who knows me better than I know myself, offered to help me select her replacement. Whoever we chose would be alone in the office a large percentage of the time, with only the company of part time typist I employed for a few hours a week. I needed a very special girl to able to cope with the solitude. After interviewing dozens of unsuitable applicants Sylvia walked into the office. She came across as a very level headed girl, not one who would let me down, nor did she seem to be the type who was obsessed with boys as she was rather ordinary looking. Yes I know that's a terrible thing for me to even think let alone say in these politically correct times. But it's always a problem when employing young women as so many of the pretty ones get pregnant just when they start being useful to me. I have experienced this situation the Midlands office. However, both Mandy and I thought Sylvia would be ideal and offered her the job.'

I paused still concerned I was talking too much.

Dr Jackson smiled at me and 'told me to me to carry on and to stop beating myself up. 'This whole incident has made me realise what a selfish bastard I am. If I had taken more notice of those around me rather than only thinking of myself, maybe things may have turned out differently.' I said. Dr Jackson didn't contradict me. Disappointed I continued.

'On my trips to the office I tried to get to know Sylvia better with the usual banal conversations we all have to illicit a response from quiet people like her, – 'never any problem with Mandy, who could talk for England.

'Where do you live'?

'Clapham'

Detecting a hint of Brummie in her voice, I asked her when did you move to London?'

'When I left school'

'Do you have a boyfriend?'

'No'.

'Do you have any family in London?

'No' I tell you, extracting teeth would have been easier. However, conversations about work were completely different. She had transformed the dreary office with a fresh coat of paint, new colourful cushions and throw on the ancient sofa and flowers on the newly polished desk. I think Mandy had worked there so long she had stopped actually seeing how drab it had become. Sylvia gave me detailed analysis of a prospective client who had made telephone enquiries about our products and suggested ideas on how to progress the sale. I was delighted with her. This duality in her aroused my curiosity and to my unfortunate eventual obsession with her.'

I felt myself beginning to get emotional, so I took a swig at the glass of water on the table to steady myself before continuing.

'Do you want a break?' a kindly Dr Jackson asked.

'No' I replied. I was just getting into my stride and didn't want to stop the flow.. On one of my visits to London -- looking out of the window high up above Paternoster Square, I spotted her going into the Cathedral. I questioned her about it when she returned and couldn't believe how animated she became talking about the beauty of the place, and telling me the difficulties Christopher Wren had had to overcome with the three monarchs he served during its construction; then how she felt God's presence there. I skipped over that last remark. 'Not sure how I feel about God, and what three monarchs?

I realised to my shame that all the years I had been coming to my London office, I had never visited the interior of Wren's masterpiece which was right on my doorstep. I decided to rectify that right away. How could I have missed it all these years? It was glorious. That fabulous blue ceiling:

The cupola the . . . I could go on for hours.

I rushed back to the office taking the stairs two at a time, -- no mean feat that, --- and gabbled away to her about what I had just seen and felt in the church, when to my surprise she planted a kiss on my cheek. I returned her kiss, this time on her lips. I know -- I should never have done that -- but she surprised me by the passion and intensity of her response.

That was the beginning of our love affair. And it was love on my part. Whereas once I had just thought she was plain to look at, I began to see her as beautiful. Her eyes were large, a green grey colour and quite hypnotic, and her passionate lovemaking never ceased to amaze me. I started to stay in town overnight to see more of her. My wife never questioned this and didn't seem the least bit concerned at my absence which made it very easy for me. I hadn't realised until that point in time just how indifferent she had become to me, and I to her. I expected Dr Jackson to say something at this point, but he didn't. Just gave me an enigmatic smile, so I carried on.

'Sylvia may have lived in the capital for many years, but as she rarely went out and didn't appear to have any friends and she knew nothing of the pleasures available in the capital. This gave me a chance to flaunt my knowledge of London to her. I'm afraid I can never miss an opportunity to 'show off' or patronise. I realise that now.' She was thrilled wherever we went, be it a smart restaurant or any of the wonderful parks: Speakers Corner, the museums, theatres and galleries that abound in the city. We enjoyed riding on the open top buses; something it had never occurred to me to do before but she had suggested it, and I loved it. We regularly went into St Paul's to marvel over the architecture and talked about Wren's courage in constructing the cupola without support. He had erected pillars that he made to look as if they were holding up the dome—which they weren't -- to assuage the fears of his doubters. When we were in the cathedral, she frequently mentioned how God had spoken to her there and told her to obey him in all things. I was so wrapped up in myself at that point that I didn't pick up the warning signs of a disturbed mind but being the selfish sod that I am, I chose to ignore what she said. On one of my visits, she told me she had joined a Christian group near her home, and they used to pray for redemption together.'

On my next visit I noticed she had nasty gashes on her arms, obviously self-inflicted and I was forced to say something as the cuts were so obvious,

I asked her if she had had an accident? She avoided answering my question by telling me about an enquiry she had had from an Arab consortium showing a great interest in our products, and I allowed her to divert me; that way I could ignore the problem of her wounds.'

Concerned I was taking up too much of Dr Jackson's time and worrying he might be thinking I was a nasty piece of work by now, which was exactly what I was beginning to think about myself and I pathetically I wanted him to like me, so I asked him did he want me to stop.

'No, no, on the contrary. I think you are beginning to understand yourself a little bit more as you speak. Please carry on' he replied.

'The following week, my world came crashing down. At five-o-clock in the morning there was a loud knocking on my door and to my surprise there were two policemen on the doorstep. I went cold thinking something had happened to my son. They wanted me to come down to the station with them.

'What on earth for?' I asked.

'To answer a few questions sir.'

'Questions? About what?' I enquired, but they wouldn't say.

When I arrived at the local police station, I was greeted by two officers from the Met waiting to escort me back to London. I was really frightened by this time, as my imagination was running riot as to what had happened, and what did it have to do with me? On reaching Bow Street station I was treated like a suspect in a serious crime. Then they told me the girl I loved was dead, and they were treating her death as suspicious and I was their prime suspect in her murder.

A private detective, who rented a room opposite mine, thought he had spotted blood seeping under the door of my office, so he had called the police to investigate. They broke the door down to find Sylvia slumped on the floor with blood gushing from her neck. Her throat had been stabbed. She was rushed to hospital, but it was too late and she died in the ambulance. I cannot begin to tell you just how devastated I felt. I was numb with shock and horrified that she should commit such a barbaric act against herself, and sick with the feeling that I would never see her again. I couldn't understand why she would do such a thing. I thought she was happy in our relationship. Typical, me putting myself centre stage as usual. I was probably the last thing she was thinking of when she killed herself.

'After an appalling grilling by the police -- they finally realised I was no murderer and that she had committed suicide they switched their line of questioning concentrating on our affair as the reason she had been driven to take her own life. Older man!-- young impressionable secretary! Oh boy, they loved that. They were positively salivating.

'Did she kill herself because you wouldn't marry her?'

'You were much older than her; fifty five years to her twenty something?' Snigger, snigger.

'Did it make you feel good having a young girl on your arm?'

They were making our affair sound dirty when to me it was beautiful. Maybe I was kidding myself, and I had taken advantage of her.

'Was she a virgin?

'Where did you seduce her? In the office, over the desk was it sir?'

'Did you force her to have sex with you?'

'NO NO NO. It wasn't like that.' I shouted, but they kept on and on in the same vein. It was all over the Evening Standard that night, -- front-page news, complete with a picture of the lover -- me. Never in my very ordinary life had I experienced such torment. I should have realised when she mentioned God talking to her and telling her how to live her life was not normal. I should have encouraged her to seek help. I told the police she had been a bit strange ever since she joined a religious group near her home in Clapham. I thought it was one of those peculiar sects that played on the emotions of susceptible girls like Sylvia.

'Or people like yourself sir?' I chose to ignore his snide remark. I told them that the leader of the group was Peter something or other. It turned out he was known to the police as a petty criminal and was fleecing the members of the group by saying he was collecting ten percent of their salaries for the homeless quoting a passage in the Bible to justify this. He was arrested.

When the police interviewed him he told them Sylvia worshiped God and had given her life to him and had promised to obey him in all things. She would die for him if that was what he wanted of her. Maybe when she was in St Paul's, He had probably told her to kill herself and join him in heaven' he told the police.'   He spoke in a flat monotone voice as if there was nothing odd in what she had done, and said 'that it had nothing to do with him. God must have told her he wanted her to join him and the heavenly host.'

'The man's an evil control freak, and is using religion to gain control and money from his followers.' the inspector told me in a much kinder tone than his previous questioning.

Her parents were located in Birmingham and came to London to answer questions about poor Sylvia. They told the police she suffered from schizophrenia, and had done so since she was a young teenager. She often refused to take her pills, and regularly ended up in hospital, and after a recent episode, she had left home and they had no idea where she might have gone. Worried because she had left her medication behind, they contacted the Salvation Army and other agencies that attempted to trace missing persons.

You can imagine what they thought of me can't you? The boss and his secretary! A classic seduction scenario was the way they viewed it.

On my way back to the Midlands I thought thank goodness they don't deliver the Evening Standard in my home town, so at least I can tell my wife in my own words what has happened without her reading some sensational journalist's version, and hoping she will understand. What I had forgotten was my DJ son Paul worked in London and had seen the Evening Standard with his Dad's face splashed all over the front page and immediately telephoned his mother to tell her of my shame. He would have enjoyed that. Needless to say Pat was incandescent with rage and humiliation when we finally met up. I think she was actually more concerned with what her friends and neighbours would have to say about my infidelity than anything she might feel.'

The usual benign look on Dr Jackson's face had changed to one of deep concern and he asked me again if I would like a break. 'No' I told him 'I want to carry on.'

'I don't think I had realised how routine my marriage had become until all this drama had occurred I told him, so when Pat decided to sue for divorce I was not surprised, nor did I care particularly -- but I did care that she wanted half of my factory as a part of her settlement as well as the house. Not being able to raise the money to pay her off, I had to sell the business. This did upset me as it had given my family a very comfortable life style over the years with the profits from the factory, and now I was going to have to start another project from scratch and I wondered if I still had the energy to do so. But, where would I go to start again? I still had the lease on the London office, but could I bear to go there again? However, it was in a prime position and had served me well over the years so I employed a cleaning firm that specialised in the removal of blood traces from the walls and floor. Another company redecorated the place: another one removed and replaced all the furniture, so when I finally plucked up courage to move back in, all traces of my previous life there had disappeared --- but had it?

I started another company again supplying computer parts again and it was going well, BUT, the office had always had a slightly spooky atmosphere. Even my 'down to earth' Mandy had told me there were spirits in the office which I dismissed.

'They were peaceful and they don't bother me, but I can hear them whispering to each other occasionally' she said in her matter of fact way. I was surprised to hear someone like her talk what I thought was rubbish. However, then Sylvia told me they spoke to her. It was inevitable that in such an ancient building there would be creaking sounds and other odd noises which could be interpreted as ghostly, so I chose to ignore both girls thinking it was just their female imaginations working overtime.. Chauvinist to the last; how wrong I was.

'Was that wise?' Dr Jackson inquired. 'Perhaps you should have called in an exorcist?' I'd almost forgotten he was there I was so absorbed in telling my tale. I was in tears by now. Feeling a bit of an idiot, I pulled myself together. I'm not one of these new men that seem to abound these days. I'm an old fashioned bloke who doesn't show his emotions.

'And the nightmares? Is this when they started?' he asked.

'Yes. Sylvia had joined the spirits in the office and makes sure I know she's there. Sometimes she pins me to my chair and I can only move when she chooses to let me go. Once I found myself on the roof overlooking St Paul's and I nearly jumped and I have no recollection of how I got there. Now she also invades my dreams calling on me to join her in paradise with God, and I'm terrified to fall asleep in case I succumb to her wishes.'

'Does this happen outside of the office? He asked in a concerned voice. 'Yes it has begun to' I told him.. 'I can't escape her. 'Please help me Dr Jackson. She is stronger than I am. I'm terrified she will eventually have her way and will kill me so I can join her. Perhaps I should just give in to her? It might be easier?'

'No, no. I'm sure I can help you rid yourself of this torment.' He assured me, but looked worried. Then he put his hand on my knee in a reassuring kind of way to calm me down. It was then that I felt Sylvia's cold hand on my shoulder steering me towards the door and out of the consulting room.

- Printed in Great Britain
by Amazon